His glance went straight to the bed when he opened the door, and his heart tightened in his chest.

Little Polly *was* still asleep, but she was sleeping peacefully in the crook of Lizzie's arm, with her small fair head resting contentedly against her shoulder.

Lizzie was awake, watching him with wary violet eyes. Unable to believe his own eyes at the scene before him, James thought that while he'd been at St Gabriel's she'd been there for his children. Once again.

Dear Reader

Having been brought up happily enough in a Lancashire mill town, where fields and trees were sparse on the landscape, I now live in the countryside and find much pleasure in the privilege of doing so. It gives me the opportunity to write about village life, with its caring communities and beautiful surroundings.

If you have been following the lives and loves of the doctors and nurses in the Cheshire village of Willowmere as the seasons come and go, I do hope that you have enjoyed my quartet of books about this close community of caring country folk. Maybe soon we will go back there once again to see what has been happening since CHRISTMAS AT WILLOWMERE, A BABY FOR THE VILLAGE DOCTOR, A SUMMER WEDDING AT WILLOWMERE, and now COUNTRY MIDWIFE, CHRISTMAS BRIDE, featuring Dr James Bartlett and new midwife Lizzie Carmichael, first appeared on the shelves.

Whatever the future holds for the beautiful village of Willowmere, I wish you all happy reading.

Abigail Gordon

The Willowmere Village Stories

COUNTRY MIDWIFE, CHRISTMAS BRIDE

BY
ABIGAIL GORDON

First published in Great Britain 2009
Harlequin Mills & Boon Limited,
Eton House, 18-24 Paradise Road, Richmond, Surrey TW9 1SR

© Abigail Gordon 2009

ISBN: 978 0 263 20941 9

Set in Times Roman 10½ on 12¾ pt
15-0909-47516

Harlequin Mills & Boon policy is to use papers that are natural,
renewable and recyclable products and made from wood grown in
sustainable forests. The logging and manufacturing process conform
to the legal environmental regulations of the country of origin.

Printed and bound in Great Britain
by CPI Antony Rowe, Chippenham, Wiltshire

Abigail Gordon loves to write about the fascinating combination of medicine and romance from her home in a Cheshire village. She is active in local affairs, and is even called upon to write the script for the annual village pantomime! Her eldest son is a hospital manager, and helps with all her medical research. As part of a close-knit family, she treasures having two of her sons living close by, and the third one not too far away. This also gives her the added pleasure of being able to watch her delightful grandchildren growing up.

Recent titles by the same author:

A SUMMER WEDDING AT WILLOWMERE*
A BABY FOR THE VILLAGE DOCTOR*
CHRISTMAS AT WILLOWMERE*
COUNTRY DOCTOR, SPRING BRIDE

The Willowmere Village Stories

CHAPTER ONE

THE first thing Lizzie Carmichael did when she arrived back at the cottage after the wedding was to ease her feet out of the elegant but not very comfortable shoes she'd worn as part of her outfit.

The second was to put the kettle on, and while it was coming to the boil there was something else she needed to do—take stock of the rented property that she'd moved into late the night before.

There'd been no time during the morning as the marriage of her friend Dr David Trelawney to Laurel Maddox, a practice nurse, had been arranged for eleven o'clock and by the time she'd sorted out some break-fast in a strange kitchen and dressed carefully for the special occasion it had been time to present herself at the church in the Cheshire village of Willowmere where the wedding was to take place.

The cottage she was renting had been David's tem-porary home while he'd been having an old house beside a beautiful lake renovated for Laurel and him-self. He'd only moved into his new home the day before, which had made her arrival a last-minute thing.

The wedding had been a delightful occasion and a pleasant introduction to the surrounding countryside, but Lizzie was in Willowmere to work. She'd transferred from St Gabriel's, the big hospital in the nearest town where she'd been employed ever since she'd qualified as a midwife, and where she'd got to know David, to take up a position in local health care that she just hadn't been able to refuse.

She'd been offered the chance to take charge of a new maternity centre that would be functioning in just one week's time in an annexe adjoining the medical practice on the main street of the village.

It would be a place where local mothers who wanted to have their babies at home would not have to rely on the services of a community midwife from the hospital some miles away, but would receive care before the birth, during the birth and in the sometimes traumatic days afterwards on a more personal level and from a much nearer source, under the supervision of a senior midwife.

The project was being funded by Lord Derringham, a local landowner who was on the board of governors at St Gabriel's, and it was due to be officially opened on the coming Friday by his wife.

Before then Lizzie would be taking a keen interest in the final arrangements that were being put in place and if necessary introducing ideas of her own, while at the same time getting to know the rest of the staff in the village practice.

The person she was going to be involved with the most was the senior partner at the practice, James Bartlett. She would be answerable to him with regard to any emergencies that occurred either before a birth or during it, and would take his advice as to whether the mother-to-be should be transferred to St Gabriel's with all speed, or just as a necessary precaution.

He'd been best man at the wedding in the old stone church and before the ceremony had begun she'd introduced herself to him. He'd seemed pleasant enough, but there hadn't been time to say much under the circumstances and she was hoping that come Monday it would be different.

She'd brought some ideas of her own with her and would be eager to discuss them with him, and at the same time be ready to take note of what he had to say from his point of view. Until then she was going to spend what was left of the weekend getting to know the place that was going to be her home for the foreseeable future.

When she'd been asked if she would take on the responsibility of the new venture she'd agreed without hesitation. Since she'd lost Richard, her husband, in a pile-up on the motorway three years ago and in the horrendous aftermath of the accident had also lost the baby that would have been their firstborn, her job had become the only thing she had left to hold on to and she gave it everything she'd got.

David had also worked at St Gabriel's, then as a registrar, before deciding to move into rural health care, and she was going to be doing the same.

When he'd mentioned that he would soon be vacating the cottage he was renting in Willowmere to start married life in the house by the lake, she'd got in touch with the letting agents and now here she was. Just across the way was one of the special attractions of the place: a flower-filled peace garden that she'd been told was the pride of the local folk who had paid to have it put there and contributed to its upkeep.

She'd sold their house after Richard and the baby had been taken from her, unable to bear seeing the nursery he'd been working on half-finished, and conscious all the time of the empty half of the bed that would always be there to remind her.

The leafy suburb where they'd lived had been left behind and she'd moved into an apartment near the hospital...*and at the same time had bought a single bed.*

It had been a modern, impersonal sort of place where she'd eaten and slept, and she would probably have stayed there for ever if the Willowmere position hadn't come up. Now she'd gone to the other extreme and was renting a small limestone cottage in an idyllic Cheshire village that she hadn't seen until the night before.

When she'd made the tea and sipped it slowly in her new surroundings, off came the suit she'd worn for the wedding, on went jeans and a sweater, and back went the long fair swathe of her hair into a ponytail as she began to unpack the boxes that held her belongings.

Once that had been accomplished it was time to find a shop as the only food in the place was a loaf she'd brought with her and a packet of cereal, which would have made rather dry eating if she hadn't noticed a farmer delivering milk to nearby properties and been able to obtain a supply from him. He'd asked if she wanted a regular delivery and she'd been quick to say yes. It would be one less thing to shop for when she was busy at the clinic.

On her way to seek out the shop, or hopefully shops, Lizzie was promising herself that if she should come across a café of some sort she was going to eat there as it was beginning to feel a long time since she'd had food at the wedding reception.

There *was* something along those lines, she discovered. The atmosphere in the Hollyhocks Tea Rooms was welcoming and the food was excellent. She would be dining there again, she decided as she left the place. As she looked around her, taking in her surroundings, she saw the doctor who'd been best man at the wedding coming towards her with a young child on either side of him. She recognised the twins, a boy and a girl that she'd already seen once that morning in the company of a dark-haired, youngish woman and an elderly lady.

James Bartlett was smiling as they drew level and as she observed the bright-eyed little girl and solemn small boy he said, 'Hello, Lizzie. You won't have met my children.' He placed the palm of his hand on top of each of their small golden heads. 'Pollyanna and Jolyon.'

'I saw them at the wedding,' she told him with an answering smile, 'but didn't realise they were yours. I suppose that having your best man's duties to perform they were with their mother.'

'We haven't got a mummy,' the boy called Jolyon said matter-of-factly. He pulled at the neck of the smart little shirt he'd worn for the wedding. 'I'm too hot, Daddy.'

'We'll be home soon,' his father told him, 'and then you can change into your play clothes.'

His sister was looking down at Lizzie's feet, now encased in comfortable casual shoes, and into the silence that followed his father's reply she said, 'Where are your blue shoes?'

James's smile was fading fast. This is just too embarrassing, he was thinking. He'd only stopped to say a brief hello to Lizzie Carmichael and within seconds Jolyon had told her about the great gap in their lives, and as Pollyanna had a thing about clomping around in Julie's shoes, no doubt she would ask Lizzie if she could try her shoes on some time.

'The shoes are at the cottage where I'm living,' Lizzie told her easily. 'They were hurting my feet.'

'I wear my mummy's shoes and pretend I'm grown up,' Pollyanna explained.

'Yes, well,' her father interrupted gently, 'perhaps we can talk about that another time, eh, Polly?' He smiled apologetically at Lizzie. 'The person you saw with the children was Jess, their nanny, and somewhere nearby would be Helen, my housekeeper. You'll no doubt get to meet them soon. Willowmere is a very friendly village.' And with his son tugging to be off and his daughter wanting to linger, he wished Lizzie a brisk goodbye and the trio went on their way.

Lizzie felt embarrassed that she'd been so presumptuous as to take for granted that the slender dark-haired woman she'd seen with the children was their mother. She wondered what had happened, and hoped she hadn't upset them. It had been an easy enough mistake to make as they'd seemed so content in the woman's company.

It was out of character, though, as after losing Richard and the baby she never presumed anything, took nothing for granted. If something good happened in her private life it was a bonus, and there hadn't been many of those over the last few years.

Meeting David and subsequently the lovely Laurel, who'd had her own bridges to build, had been one, and she hoped that one day she might have the pleasure of seeing the young bride at her maternity clinic. But there would be plenty of time for that, and she, Lizzie, would be around for all of it as she intended to settle permanently in Willowmere, circumstances permitting.

She'd been going to ask James about the shops in the village but had been sidetracked by the children, and now as she looked around her Lizzie saw that there was no need to have enquired. They were all there on the main street, one after the other, starting with the post office at one end, an attractive delicatessen next to it, then the usual butcher's, bakery, greengrocer's and the rest, all of them with a quaint individuality of their own that set them apart from the usual shopping facilities of the modern age.

As James walked up the drive of Bracken House, his detached property next to the surgery, with the children skipping along in front, he was wishing that his introduction to the latest member of health care in the village had been more dignified.

Theirs was going to be essentially a working relationship and already Polly and Jolly in their innocence had turned it into something less official, and *he'd* ended up reciting his domestic arrangements as if by some remote chance Lizzie might want to hear them.

She was an unknown quantity and that was how he would like it to stay until Monday morning. Time then to see if the bright star of the maternity unit at St Gabriel's was going to be the right one for Willowmere and the nearby rural communities.

He was well pleased that home births were being highlighted through the generosity of Lord Derringham, and knew that his lordship would have insisted that his project be properly staffed, and he supposed that what little he'd seen of the newcomer so far was reassuring.

She was in her early thirties, according to the information he'd been given, which made her five or so years younger than himself, and was unattached which he supposed could mean anything. But her having moved into the tiny cottage that David had been renting seemed to indicate that as well as being unattached Lizzie Carmichael lived alone...though he was presuming, of course.

At the opposite side of the surgery there was an annexe built from sturdy local stone, as were most of the buildings in the village, and the new maternity unit was taking shape inside.

The annexe had served various purposes over the years. At one time it had housed James's sister, Anna, who was now working out in Africa with her husband, Glenn.

After years of separation, they had married in January and were finally living their dream, and James was delighted for them.

The inside of the annexe had now been gutted and the whole structure altered to accommodate the needs of the expectant mothers who would be attending the centre, and now the woman whose calling brought her in touch with other women's babies all the time had arrived in Willowmere.

When Lizzie went upstairs to bed that night the shoes she'd worn for the wedding were where she'd taken them off. She remembered the interest that James's little girl had shown in them, which she supposed wasn't surprising. They had high heels, open, strappy fronts, and were made out of pale blue leather to match the suit she'd been wearing. They'd been an extravagance of the kind that she rarely allowed herself and hadn't been all that comfortable when it came to wearing them, but to the small Pollyanna they must have seemed quite exciting if she was into putting her small feet into her mother's old shoes.

It was the evening of what had been a mellow Sunday in September. James had read the children a bedtime story and as their eyelids were beginning to droop he was about to go downstairs for a quiet hour with a new medical journal that he'd been trying to find time to read when through the window on the landing he saw the midwife walking alongside the river that ran behind the house and the practice.

Lizzie was alone and there was a solitariness about her that was so unmistakable that he forgot how he hadn't wanted to be involved with her out of working hours and he opened the back door of Bracken House and called, 'Hi, there, it's a beautiful night. Are you getting used to your new surroundings?'

She halted beside the fast-flowing river as he walked down to his garden gate.

'Yes,' she replied. 'So far I'm acquainted with Willow Lake because of David and Laurel, have dined in the excellent tea rooms, shopped on the main street, and now I'm exploring the river bank, but not for long as I intend to have an early night. It's been hectic moving here at the last minute and I want to be on top form for tomorrow.'

'So you haven't had anyone to help you with the move?'

'Er, no,' she said, seeming mildly surprised at the question. 'It was no problem, though. I'm used to sorting out my own affairs.'

'Would you like to come in for a cold drink or a coffee?'

She hesitated for a moment, then said politely, 'Yes, thank you. It is rather warm. A cold drink would be nice.'

He nodded and opened the gate that gave him access to the river bank, and as he led the way into the house Lizzie was still wishing she could act naturally with this man who was going to be a close colleague in the days and weeks to come.

Maybe it was because he was so impressive to look at, or perhaps she wasn't as confident as she'd thought she was over her new appointment. Whatever it was, he was giving her the opportunity to get to know him better and she supposed she may as well accept the offer of some light refreshment.

The house, when she went inside, was impressive by anyone's standards, pleasant, roomy, with children's clutter in a couple of the rooms. Pointing to doors down a side passage, James said, 'That is my housekeeper's domain during the week, a sitting room and bedroom where she can do her own thing. At weekends Helen usually goes home. She has one of the new apartments further along the river bank.'

Lizzie nodded. She was looking around her and thinking that the cottage she was renting would fit into a corner of Bracken House, yet it was big enough for her needs in the solitary life she'd chosen.

He'd gone into the kitchen to get the drinks and while he was there her glance was fixed on a photograph of a smiling raven-haired woman holding a tiny baby in each arm. It had to be the mother, she thought, and the infants had to be the children who had both captivated her and aroused her curiosity the day before.

When James brought a jug of home-made lemonade in, he saw the direction of her gaze but made no comment, and after her wrong assumption when she'd had the nanny down for the mother, Lizzie was not going to risk a repeat of that kind of thing.

'You will have seen the new centre from the outside, no doubt,' James said, steering the conversation towards less personal channels. 'What do you think of it?'

She smiled and he thought she should do it more often. 'What I've seen so far is impressive. I haven't met Lord Derringham, but from what I've heard he isn't sparing any expense.

'I've also been told that as well as it being a thank-you gesture to the practice for the care that David and Laurel gave to his son when he had an accident up on the moors, his lordship has a young family of his own and is keen to see first-class maternity care in Willowmere and the surrounding villages.'

'That is correct *and* the reason why you are here.'

'Mmm. I'm known as workaholic and I suppose it's true. Midwifery is the most rewarding of occupations and comes with the responsibility of bringing new life into the world carefully and safely for the sake of the newborn and its mother.'

She finished her drink and was getting up to go, feeling that she'd flown the flag enough for her love of the job. James could have invited her in solely to be hospitable and she'd been going on like someone with a one-track mind, yet wasn't that what she was? There was nothing else in her life to wrap around with loving care, just the mothers and babies that came and went.

'Thanks for the drink,' she said as she stepped into the dusk. 'Until tomorrow, then?'

He nodded. 'Yes, until tomorrow.'

* * *

As he put out the empty bottles for Bryan Timmins, the farmer who delivered the milk each morning, and then locked up for the night, James was glad that he'd invited Lizzie in for a drink.

He'd been wrong to think that Monday would have been early enough to get to know the newcomer. He'd got a new slant on her in the short time they'd been together and was going to feel more relaxed in her company when they met up again in the morning.

Her devotion to the job was clear to see and would be most welcome, but he was just a bit concerned that it seemed to have such a hold on her, as if there was nothing else that mattered. Yet he could be wrong about that. She could have lots of other interests that she hadn't mentioned, as during their first conversation of any length Lizzie was hardly going to recite chapter and verse all the things that made up her life. They were her affair and hers alone.

He hadn't told her he was a widower, had he, though he wasn't sure why. He made no secret of it in his dealings with either of the sexes, yet with her the words had stuck in his throat, and even if she was the least curious of women, he would expect her to wonder why his children had no mother.

No doubt Lizzie would find out soon enough that he was the most sought-after catch in Willowmere, with lots of experience in dodging the net.

Monday morning came and at Bracken House it was time to get ready for the children's first day of a new school year. Jess had arrived with her usual promptness and as she gave the children their breakfast and sorted out the new uniforms that went with the new term, Helen was busy in the kitchen, putting together a packed lunch for Jolyon, who didn't like school dinners.

It was as James came down the stairs, showered and dressed in one of the smart suits that he wore at the practice, that the phone rang. When he picked it up a voice that was beginning to sound familiar spoke in his ear.

'James, forgive me for bothering you, but you're the only person I know in this place,' Lizzie cried frantically. 'There's a bull at my kitchen window. I'd left it open and it's staring at me while it's munching one of the plants on the window sill. I've never been so near one before and I'm scared. I don't know what to do.'

'It will belong to Bryan Timmins, who delivers your milk,' he said as he watched Helen put his breakfast on the table. 'I'll be right over. Keep the door shut, Lizzie, and I'll phone Bryan to come and get it while I'm on my way.'

'Please don't be long,' she begged. 'It's nearly finished eating the plant and I'm scared what it's going to do next.'

'I'm coming,' he promised, and before the children got wind of it and wanted to come he was striding swiftly down the main street to where the cottage stood beside the peace garden, which he was relieved to see had so far escaped the wanderer's appetite.

When Lizzie opened the door to him, wrapped in a tightly belted robe with hair hanging limp from the shower, she said anxiously, 'It's still there! I don't know what to do, James!'

'All right,' he soothed as he went through to the kitchen. 'Bryan is on his way. We'll soon have it back where it belongs.' He smiled when he saw the unwelcome visitor. 'It isn't a bull, Lizzie. She's just a harmless cow from his dairy herd that has wandered through the broken fence at the bottom of your garden. I'll point her in the right direction while we're waiting for Bryan to show up.'

He opened the back door of the cottage, went outside and herded the obedient cow towards the gap in the fence.

As Lizzie watched in complete mortification he stopped and looked down at his feet and she saw that Daisy had left a calling card. James had stepped in a cow pat.

With his expression giving nothing away, he continued herding the intruder towards the field from where it had come, and Lizzie didn't know whether to laugh or cry.

What a ghastly beginning to her first day at the village practice, she was thinking. It was almost time to put in an appearance and she was only half-dressed, hadn't had any breakfast, and her knight in shining armour was going to have to change his trousers, which were spattered around the bottoms, and clean up what looked like a pair of hand-made shoes.

At that moment the farmer appeared and apologised for his animal's wanderings. 'Daisy wouldn't harm you,' he said. 'Will you forgive her for the intrusion on to your property if I mend your fence?'

'Yes,' she agreed weakly.

On receiving her agreement, he went to take charge of the cow and when James returned to the cottage she said awkwardly, 'I'll pay for the dry cleaning and any damage to your shoes.'

'Forget it,' he said easily. 'That's what country life is all about. I'm going to go and get changed and will be hoping that my breakfast hasn't dried up in the oven. What about you? Have you eaten?'

'Not yet, no,' she said uncomfortably. 'I'm so sorry for making such a fuss. The thought of being late on my first day at the clinic doesn't bear thinking about, so I'm going to grab a slice of toast and then get dressed…and thank you for coming to my aid. I don't usually freak out like that, I can assure you.'

'I'm sure you don't,' he told her, 'but even a harmless cow can seem menacing when close to. Bye for now, Lizzie,' he said. He paused with his hand on the latch of the garden gate. 'Make sure you have a proper breakfast, not just a piece of toast. There's no rush. The mothers-to-be aren't queuing up for your services yet, so no need for further panic.'

He'd been smiling as he'd said it, but as she went back inside Lizzie wondered just how much James had meant it. Had he seen the episode with the cow as a confidence crisis on her part? If he had, she would have to remind him that she was here to see babies safely into the world. The animal kingdom was someone else's responsibility.

Lizzie ignored James's advice not to skip breakfast and had just a glass of milk before quickly drying her hair and then putting it in a long plait that swung smoothly against her shoulders. It was hardly the height of fashion but was soon done and time was something she hadn't got if she wasn't going to be late at the clinic.

Uniform, tights and shoes were soon on, followed by a swift application of make-up, and she was on her way, carrying the case that went everywhere with her when on duty.

She would be hungry before the morning was over, she thought as she hurried along the main street, but it was an important day in her life and she was not going to be late for it.

Every time she thought about the cow at her window her face burned. The animal hadn't got horns, she should have known it wasn't a bull, but she would still have felt most uneasy at finding it there.

There were children on the street, all heading for the village school and the first day of term. Ahead of her she could see James's twins skipping along beside the nanny and she wondered what she did for the rest of the day during term time once she'd seen them safely inside.

When James stepped out of the front door of Bracken House he saw her coming up the street with the brisk grace of a woman who was in charge of her life, and thought whimsically that there was no resemblance to the dishevelled person who'd begged him to come quickly and get rid of her unwelcome visitor earlier that morning.

This was the real Lizzie Carmichael, he thought, dressed in the standard blue uniform of her calling, with hair swept back into a plait of all things and sensible flat shoes on her feet that bore no resemblance to the ones that Polly had admired.

His daughter hadn't been the only one who had noticed the wedding guest in pale blue elegance. Though his interest had been only mild curiosity until she'd introduced herself as the person appointed by St Gabriel's to be in charge of the new maternity clinic. Since then it seemed as if she was everywhere he turned.

'Well done,' he said in a low voice when she was near enough to hear him, 'but you haven't eaten, have you? You can't have, there hasn't been time.'

'No. I've had a glass of milk, though.'

'I see. So shall we go inside? I'm sure you must be eager to see where you're going to be working. Once you've had a good look round and I've introduced you to the surgery staff I suggest you pop across to my place and Helen will make you a pot of tea and a bacon sandwich, or whatever you're used to at this time of day. I think we can manage without you for half an hour or so.'

Lizzie could feel her colour rising. She wasn't used to being looked after. He'd already done her one favour with regard to the cow. She was uncomfortably aware that he'd changed his suit, and that his shoes had got back their shine, both chores he could have done without on a Monday morning before he'd had his breakfast. And hadn't there been just a hint of patronage in his last comment?

But she could hardly refuse the offer in the circumstances and so she said in the same polite tone as on the night before when she'd been invited into his home for a drink, 'That is very kind. An offer I can't refuse.'

He nodded. 'That's good, then. So shall we start the day? I told the receptionists last week not to make me any appointments for the first hour this morning so that I can be available to show you around, and once that's done I'll leave you to get acquainted with the new maternity clinic.

'You will have your own receptionist. We have four at present, and one of those will be transferred so that your patients can go straight to maternity care without visiting the surgery, unless you decide they need to.

'Although yours will be a separate unit, a communicating door has been made between the two places to save time and energy, but the only person you will be answerable to in the surgery will be me.'

Lizzie nodded, trying to force the morning's embarrassing events from her mind. She was determined that from now on James would only see the calm, collected, professional Lizzie Carmichael, and nothing more.

CHAPTER TWO

WHEN the door swung open and James stepped back to let her precede him into the building Lizzie knew immediately that she was going to be happy there, not just in the pristine, well-appointed rooms with every facility for antenatal and postnatal care, but in Willowmere itself.

She had found the perfect combination in this pretty Cheshire village where outside late summer was starting to turn the colour of the leaves on the trees and inside was the place where she was going to revel in the role that she'd been asked to play.

There was a waiting room painted in cream, beige and gold, with a honey wool carpet to match. Plenty of comfortable chairs that were not too low for heavily pregnant mothers to rise up from were arranged in rows, and in a corner was a reception desk.

Through a door at the end was a consulting room where she would interview new patients and listen to the problems of those already registered with the clinic.

Next to it there was a room divided into cubicles where she, and James if necessary, would check on the

progress of the babies and the general health of the
mothers-to-be. It was equipped with scales, a medicine
cupboard for on-the-spot medication if needed, and
various other items that her practised eye had noted,
such as comfy cotton gowns for examination time and
disposable sheets, plus a pile of glossy magazines to leaf
through while waiting. Through another door were hand
washbasins and toilets.

'So what's the verdict?' James asked when she'd
observed everything without comment.

'Wonderful!' she exclaimed, eyes bright with enthusiasm. 'It's so relaxing and clean looking. Who were the
brains behind all this?'

'The hospital hired a firm to do the make-over, but
Lady Derringham had the last word on the décor and po-
sitioning of the facilities. You will be meeting her on
Friday at the official opening.

'You might have noticed that there hasn't been room
to put in any kitchen space for your needs, but we have
that kind of thing in the surgery and you will be welcome to use it whenever you want.'

He was smiling. 'And now do you think you can
drag yourself away while I introduce you to the people
on the other side of the communicating door?'

'Yes, of course,' she replied, and went to meet Ben
Allardyce, a well-known paediatric surgeon, who was
standing in for his wife, Georgina, the only female GP
in the practice, while she was on maternity leave.

And then there was Gillian, one of the two practice
nurses, holding the fort while Laurel was on her hon-

eymoon, and Sarah Martin, a pretty, curvy girl and the youngest of the receptionists, who would be transferring to the new maternity centre.

Elaine Ferguson, the practice manager, came and shook hands and the good feeling that Lizzie had felt when she stepped into the place was still there.

Life without Richard and the child she'd been carrying would have been an empty thing if it hadn't been for her job, she thought. Maybe here in Willowmere she might find a different kind of solace in friendly folk and delightful surroundings as everyone was making her most welcome.

The one who stood out amongst them the most, however, was the man who was now speaking in a low voice for her ears only. 'It's half past nine, my first patient is due any moment. I'm going to take you to Helen for a belated breakfast.'

Lizzie nodded with head averted, afraid to speak in case the tears that were threatening began to roll down her cheeks. She just wasn't used to this, she thought unevenly. It would be easy to get to like it, and then what?

Loneliness had become a way of life and it was partly her own fault, but it had its advantages. By not ever getting close to anyone again she'd avoided any more pain. So was this beautiful Cheshire village going to make her see life differently? Did she want to be side-tracked into a kind of lifestyle she hadn't bargained for?

As James's middle-aged housekeeper plied her with eggs, bacon, hot buttered toast and a pot of tea Helen said chattily, 'So, my dear, you're the midwife who is coming to work in the new maternity clinic at the practice.'

'Yes, that's me,' she said, smiling across at her.

'James is highly delighted at the new arrangement,' Helen informed her. 'His life revolves around health care in the village. It comes second only to his love for his children and his sister. I kept house for his parents when he and Anna were young until I went to live in Canada to be with my daughter while her children were small, but now they're grown up I've come back. I was homesick and James needed some help in the house, so here we all are.

'Jess, their nanny, is also a classroom assistant during term time, which works well as she's at school the same hours as the children and is available all the time during the holidays.

'We leave James to it at the weekends to give him some quality time with Polly and Jolly. All those who love him would like to see him married again but he shows no inclination to put anyone in their mother's place and seems happy enough. But I mustn't go rambling on, though you'll find out soon enough that he lost his wife in a car crash when the children were just a few weeks old.'

That was how she'd lost Richard, Lizzie thought. How weird that they should have both lost their partners in similar circumstances. Obviously all Willowmere would know what happened to James's wife. It was that kind of place.

Not so with her situation. Most of the staff who'd

been at St Gabriel's when her own life had been torn apart had moved on. Any that remained had their own lives to lead, their own peaks and valleys to cope with, and that was how she'd wanted it to stay.

As she made her way back to the practice building, having thanked Helen most sincerely for taking away her hunger pangs, she avoided the surgery and went straight to the clinic. She was still trying to come to terms with what Helen had told her about James. How he was bringing up his children as a single father, and providing a high standard of health care for Willowmere at the same time.

That being so, it was to be expected that there wouldn't be much opportunity for a life of his own and it could be one of the reasons why he'd never remarried. Though for most people who found themselves alone the need for someone to fill the gap outweighed every other consideration, but not in his case, it would seem, and neither was it so for her.

Her face was warming again at the memory of how she'd dragged him away from his breakfast that morning because of the placid Daisy's appearance at her kitchen window.

Presumably he'd eaten when he'd got back, but she wouldn't have been the only one who'd had to put a spurt on timewise, and then after all that he'd taken the trouble to arrange for Helen to cook breakfast for her.

Their lives were similar in some ways, she thought as she let herself into the clinic once more, but vastly different in others. Whatever his problems, James's life sounded as if it was full and rewarding, except for the one big gap of a loving wife and mother, and if what his housekeeper had said was correct, those who cared about him would like to see the blank space filled.

But the length of time it remained empty was often an indication of the depth of the loss. It brought with it a steadfast loving faithfulness that was a barrier to any other relationships.

Memories of Richard were so clear and tender there was no way she wanted any other man to hold her close in the night or sit across the table from her at mealtimes. As for the baby she'd lost, there were moments when she envied a radiant mother as she placed her child in her arms, but it was also like balm to her soul every time she brought a newborn safely into the world.

Unlike the man in the surgery next door, her life was only half-full, but she'd learned to live with that, she always told herself when she was feeling low. Though was half a life better than none, she sometimes wondered.

It seemed that James lived by a different set of rules from hers. In the middle of his busy life he had found time to show her an impersonal sort of kindness that was heart-warming, and she was going to repay him by making his dream of a maternity clinic in the village an efficient reality.

She spent the rest of the morning unpacking deliveries of stationery and medical supplies, and at lunchtime went across to the Hollyhocks Tea Rooms for a quick bite. It was a luxury she knew she would probably have to forego when things got busy at the unit, but she had the next few days to settle in at her own pace before the grand opening on Friday, when as well as the Derringhams some of the bigwigs from St Gabriel's would be there.

James appeared again just before his afternoon surgery was about to commence and said, 'How's it going? I thought we might have seen you at lunchtime. If you remember, I said that you're welcome to join us whenever you feel the need.'

'Yes, I know,' she told him, 'but I thought you might be feeling you've seen enough of me for one day.'

'I'm not with you,' he said, and then laughed. 'Ah, you mean Daisy. Don't give it another thought. My mother was born and bred in the countryside but she was nervous if they came too near, and she would never go within a mile of a pig sty.'

He was making it up as he went along because he didn't want this newcomer with hair in a long golden plait and a clear violet gaze to have any reason to regret having moved to the beautiful village where he'd been born.

She'd positively sparkled when she'd seen the new clinic for the first time, but for the rest of it she seemed rather subdued and he wondered what went on in her life.

Yet did that matter? If Lizzie was as good as she was said to be, he couldn't ask for more and with that in mind he said, 'Would you be prepared to come back this evening for a couple of hours while I put you in the picture regarding our present antenatal arrangements and pass on to you the medical notes of the expectant mothers at presently under our care, who will be transferred from the surgery to the new clinic?

'As you know, we are a doctor and nurse short at the moment, with David and Laurel on honeymoon, which means that I have no spare time during the day,' he explained, 'otherwise I wouldn't break into your evening. We could have met at my place or yours, I suppose, but as a matter of protocol I wouldn't want patients' records to leave the surgery.'

'I don't mind in the least,' she said immediately. 'I have plenty of time on my hands. I've been going for a stroll and then having an early night, so I'm not going to be missing anything.'

It was there again, he thought. A solitariness that was so different from his own life. He was surrounded by people he cared for, and who cared for him.

If time for himself was hard to come by, so what? The children were happy and healthy, and the pain of losing Julie was lessening as the years went by, yet it would never go away completely because she wasn't going to see her children grow up, and that was always what hurt the most.

Lizzie was waiting for him to finish what he'd started and bringing his mind back to the present he said, 'Would eight o'clock suit you? The children will be asleep by then. I don't think they'll need much persuasion as the first day of a new school year is always exhausting for everyone concerned, and Helen is there to keep an eye on them.'

He was checking the time. The waiting room was filling up.

'Yes, eight o'clock will be fine,' she told him.

'Right, I'll see you, then,' he said briskly, and off he went, hoping that the pride of St Gabriel's maternity services wasn't thinking that he was overdoing the getting-to-know-you routine.

As Lizzie walked home in the late afternoon she was wishing that she hadn't been quite so eager to fall in with James's suggestion that they meet again that evening. Anything to do with the new clinic was of paramount importance to her, but she felt as if she needed to get her breath back after such an eventful day of ups and downs, the downs issuing from her continuing mortification over the cow episode, and the ups a deep satisfaction with the arrangements of the clinic. Not to mention what had happened when she'd gone to the Hollyhocks Tea Rooms for her lunch.

Emma, the usually rosy-cheeked wife of the partnership who owned the place, had said hesitantly, 'Is it you that's going to be in charge of the new baby clinic that's opening on Friday?'

'Yes, it's me,' Lizzie replied, wondering what was coming next.

'I think I'm pregnant,' Emma had said. 'I've done a test that I bought from the chemist and it was positive. So can I come to see you?'

'Of course,' she'd said, smiling at her across the counter. 'That's what I'm going to be there for. Is it your first baby?'

'Yes, and we just can't believe it. We've been married a long time and had almost given up hope.'

'So how about coming in on Friday after the opening and being my first patient?'

'I'd love to be that! Simon is over the moon. He's been getting all the recipes mixed up this morning, so watch out for salt instead of sugar in your apple crumble,' she'd warned laughingly.

On the whole the ups had far outweighed the downs and she wanted it to stay that way, but there had been a slight lift of the eyebrow when she'd impulsively told James that she had plenty of time on her hands, as if he found it hard to believe that anyone could be in that position, and the last thing she wanted was to arouse his curiosity.

She was getting on with her life the best way she knew how, and providing a useful service to the community took away some of the loneliness that rightly or wrongly she didn't confide to anyone.

But she'd committed herself to returning to the clinic that evening and when she gave her word about anything, she kept it.

The children were full of their first day at school when James came in from the surgery that evening, or rather Pollyanna was. Jolyon was his usual self and his contribution to the discussion was that their new teacher had said he had a funny name.

'She said unusual, not funny,' Pollyanna corrected him, 'and that she thought it was very nice.'

'It means the same,' he protested, ignoring the last bit, 'and why isn't any other kid called the same as me, Daddy? Why am I not called Sam or Tom?'

Jess had given them their evening meal and was standing in the doorway of the dining room ready to leave, but she paused and said in a low voice, 'The teacher was just trying to be nice, but as we know Jolly has a mind of his own.'

James nodded and, taking Jolyon to one side, said to him, 'There was a boy in my class at school who didn't like his name because he was the only one who had it, but as he grew older he began to change his mind because everyone was envious that he had such a super name and wished that theirs wasn't Sam or Tom.'

'What was he called?' Polly chipped in.

'His name sounded very much like yours, Jolyon, but not quite. He was called Joel.'

Apparently satisfied with the explanation, Jolyon nodded his small blond head and ran off to play, and as he ate his solitary meal James was smiling at the difference in his children. Polly accepted everything as it came her way, but not so her brother—he had to know the whys and wherefores before he was happy.

When he arrived at the new clinic there was no sign of Lizzie and he thought that maybe she wasn't the eager beaver that she'd seemed to be earlier, but when he glanced across the road in the dusk to where the ancient village church stood he saw a flash of colour amongst the gravestones that surrounded it and seconds later she was coming towards him through the lychgate.

'There are some really old graves in the churchyard, aren't there?' she commented, and wondered why a shadow passed over his face. But, of course, maybe his wife's was one of the newer ones, she thought, although she hadn't seen it if it was. So less said about that the better. Changing the subject, she asked politely, 'Have the children enjoyed their first day back at school?'

'Er...up to a point in Jolyon's case,' he said wryly. 'Pollyanna was her usual happy self, but her brother is not so easily pleased. They had a new teacher who apparently commented on his name in what appears to have been the nicest possible way, but he took it to mean that she didn't like it. He and I had a little chat and it was sorted.'

She was smiling. 'It is a fact that young children want to be the same as their friends and don't want to be different, but if they have an unusual name, they often come to like it as they get older. My name isn't unusual but I have had to answer to many forms of it over the years, such as Beth, Liz, Bet and Lizzie, which is the one that has stuck, though in truth the one I like best is Elizabeth, my given name.'

'What do your family call you?'

'I have no family, but when I did have they called me Lizzie.'

'You have no family at all?' he questioned in amazed disbelief, so much aware of his own blessings he felt guilty.

'No,' she said steadily, and her tone told him that was the end of the discussion, as did the fact that she was observing the pile of patients records on the reception desk in the waiting room and settling herself on one of the chairs that were placed in neat rows across the room.

As he came to sit beside her Lizzie said, 'I think the seating arrangements in here have too much uniformity. I want it to be that while the mothers-to-be are waiting their turn they can chat to each other easily, with the chairs scattered around the room. So if it's all right with you, I'm going to rearrange them. It is very important for women to be able to share their fears and excitement, *and* their problems, with each other, especially if they are first-time patients taking what can be a scary step into the unknown.'

'It's fine by me,' he told her. 'You are the one who is going to be in charge of this place. My function will be to be there if you need me. I would only interfere if I thought it absolutely necessary, and with your record of excellence at St Gabriel's having preceded you, I can't see that ever happening.

'But, Lizzie, don't let this place take over your life completely,' he continued, and couldn't believe what he was saying when the fates had sent to Willowmere someone as dedicated to health care as the woman sitting beside him. 'There are lots of things to do in the village, people to get to know, beautiful places to explore, as well as looking after the pregnant women in our midst.

'So why don't I take you to Willowmere's only pub, The Pheasant, when we've finished here? It will give you the opportunity to socialise a little.'

It was there again, Lizzie was thinking. He was picking up on the emptiness of her life and she didn't want him to be concerned about her. For one thing, she hardly knew the man, and for another, apart from during working hours when they would have to be in contact, she wanted to be left to get on with her life, such as it was.

But James was putting himself out to make her feel welcome when he must have plenty of other things to do in his busy life, and it would seem ungrateful to refuse his suggestion, so she said, 'Yes, if you're sure that you have the time.'

'Yes, I'm sure,' he said calmly, and, passing her the first lot of patients' notes, began to explain who they were and what they would be expecting from her.

When they'd finished going through them Lizzie said, 'It would seem that there will shortly be another name to add to these.'

'I'm not with you,' he commented.

'I went to the café across the road at lunchtime and Emma asked for an appointment as she's done the pregnancy test from the chemist and it showed positive. So we've arranged for her to be the first patient at the clinic after the opening on Friday.'

'Emma pregnant!' he exclaimed. 'Wonderful! She and Simon have wanted to start a family for a long time. She had a miscarriage when they were first married and there has been nothing since.'

'So I will have to take great care of her, won't I?'

'Yes, you will,' he agreed, 'and now am I going to take you for that drink?'

'Er…won't your housekeeper wonder where you've got to?' she said with an unmistakable lack of enthusiasm, and he wanted to laugh. He could think of two or three unattached female members of the community, and one who was already in a relationship, who would have jumped at the idea, but not so this one, it seemed.

'No, not at all,' he assured her perversely. 'But to put your mind at rest, I'll call at the house before we go and let her know where I will be if she needs me.' And Lizzie had to go along with that.

The Pheasant was crowded and when they walked in various people greeted James and observed his companion with curiosity, which was satisfied somewhat as he introduced her as the new community midwife who was joining him for a drink to celebrate the opening of the new clinic.

By the time they'd found a couple of seats and James had fought his way to the bar and back, Lizzie was feeling more relaxed, grateful for the way he had introduced her into the socialising throng without causing her embarrassment.

At the same time she was telling herself if she was going to fit into the life of the village she was going to have to start living again, and after three years of shutting herself away from everything but her job, it was not going to be easy.

James was observing her expression and almost as if he'd read her mind he said, 'That wasn't so bad after all, was it? Everyone was listening when I introduced you, so now they all know who you are.'

'If you say so,' she agreed. 'You know the people here better than I do. Have you always lived in Willowmere?'

'Yes. My father was in charge of the practice before me, but after my mother died he began to fail and my sister, Anna, gave up all her plans for the future and came home from university to help me during a very difficult time. Thankfully her life is now back on course again.'

He was speaking about his family in the hope that she would mention the absence of hers, but the ploy wasn't working. Lizzie wore a wedding ring, he'd noticed, but there was no husband around.

Maybe she was divorced and that was the reason for her reticence, yet a marriage break-up seemed as nothing to some people, but it had to be a daunting experience in many ways.

He had his children and his sister in his life, and if what she'd said was true, the woman sitting opposite had no one. Small wonder that she wasn't the life and soul of the party, but he needed to bear in mind that she'd only arrived in Willowmere a few days ago.

It was dark when they left The Pheasant with no moon above and James said, 'I'm going to walk you home, Lizzie, and will want to see you safely inside before I leave you.'

'I'll be fine,' she protested.

'Yes, I'm sure you will, but nevertheless that is what I'm going to do.'

'All right, then…and thanks,' she said awkwardly without any social grace.

They walked in silence, past the shops all shuttered for the night, then skirted the single-storey village school built from the familiar limestone, and then the peace garden came in to sight, with the cottage across the way.

He watched in silence as she unlocked the door and stepped over the threshold and when she turned to face him, said, 'Goodnight, Lizzie. Make sure you lock up when I've gone.'

She nodded mutely and watched until he disappeared from sight, then did as he'd said, and when that was done she sat on the bottom step of the stairs and wept because a stranger's concern was breaking down her defences.

From what she'd seen of James so far he seemed to be that kind of person, considerate and caring towards everyone, herself included as the latest addition to the health care of his beloved village, and she didn't want it to be like that. She didn't want to have feelings in the half of her life that was empty, because with feelings came weakness and she needed to be strong to face each day.

As he walked home, James was telling himself that he had enough responsibilities in his life without attempting to take on the emotional burden that Lizzie obviously wanted to keep private. She was going to be the right one for the job and that was all that mattered.

It was Friday afternoon and Lady Derringham was about to cut the tape that had been placed across the entrance to the new maternity clinic in front of those assembled for the occasion, which included her husband, the chairman of the primary care trust for the area, dignitaries from St Gabriel's, and Lizzie and James.

Lizzie could see Emma from the tea rooms at the front of the crowd that had gathered to watch the opening ceremony, and she smiled. Emma had been to see James and her booking-in appointment was arranged for that day.

Shortly she would have her photograph taken as the first patient to attend the clinic. It would be open for business and Lizzie's feeling of being on the edge of things would disappear.

James was observing her and noting that today she was well and truly in her midwife mode, immaculate in the blue uniform of her calling, hair in the golden plait and eyes bright with the significance of the moment.

As his glance met hers he decided that the other side of her personality that had seemed so solitary and withdrawn must have been a figment of his imagination. She was calm, confident, unfazed by the ceremonial aspect of the gathering...and content.

The scissors had snipped, the tape was cut, and her ladyship was saying, 'I now declare the Derringham Maternity Clinic well and truly open.' And as she stepped inside they all trooped in after her.

As James came to stand beside Lizzie he said, 'You are happy today, aren't you?'

'Yes,' she replied. 'More than I've been in a long time.'

He nodded. 'That's good.'

CHAPTER THREE

THE crowd had gone, the officials from St Gabriel's had driven off in their cars. Only Lord and Lady Derringham remained and Lizzie was discovering that Olivia Derringham's interest in the clinic was not going to be a passing thing.

As the person who was going to be in charge she had been expressing her appreciation of the facilities that had been provided and the uplifting design of the place and Olivia said, 'If you think it would be all right, I'd like to volunteer to come in for a couple of mornings each week to give what assistance I can, even if it is only to make tea, help out the receptionist and perhaps settle the patients in the cubicles as they wait to be seen.'

'That's a very kind offer,' Lizzie told her, slightly taken aback. 'I'll speak with James, but I'm sure it would be fine. Most of the time I will be on my own, except for the receptionist who is being transferred from the surgery, and I'm presuming that it will be quite busy, with expectant mothers from surrounding villages transferring to this clinic as well as those from Willowmere.

I've been told that extra staff will be brought in if needed, but the hospital trust is waiting to see what the workload turns out to be first. So I would much appreciate help from someone like yourself.'

Olivia Derringham nodded and went on to say, 'I suppose you know that we have donated the clinic as our way of thanking two members of the village practice who I believe are on honeymoon at the moment. I would have liked them to be here, as what they did for our son—you know he had a nasty fall while on a sponsored walk that they were also taking part in—was something that my husband and I won't forget. But when they made their wedding plans they had no idea that the clinic would be finished so soon and urged us to go ahead with the opening rather than there be any delay, so here we are, and you'll let me know about helping out then?'

'Certainly. Thank you for your kind offer of support, Lady Derringham.'

'Lizzie, the name is Olivia. I was working in a burger bar when I met His Lordship, and now I need to remind my husband, who is deep in conversation with Dr Bartlett, that we need to be home in time for nursery tea.'

'You look somewhat stunned,' James commented when they'd gone. 'What gives?'

'I don't know if you would agree to this, James, but Her Ladyship has offered to help in the clinic for a couple of mornings each week.'

He frowned. 'But she isn't trained!'

'Not doing midwifery. She's volunteered her time to

help out in Reception where needed, make tea and coffee, and make sure the patients are comfortable. In other words, she's offering to be a general dogsbody.'

'Amazing!'

She laughed. 'She has no airs and graces. They met in a burger bar, of all places. She worked there. Don't you think it's rather romantic? She is a very nice woman. I'm sure we'd get on well.'

'Yes, I'm sure you would,' he agreed. 'Well, let me look into this and I'll let you know shortly.' Lizzie smiled and he thought how she looked bright-eyed and happy now, but he knew that no matter how he tried to tell himself otherwise, somewhere not too far away was the other Lizzie, subdued and wanting to be left alone. But as he'd told himself several times since they'd met, that was her affair.

'Until their son's accident and David and Laurel's involvement in it, we only saw the Derringhams rarely,' he explained. 'This is a new dimension her wanting to help in the clinic, and it is very commendable.'

'Where do they live?'

'At Kestrel Court, a large place on the way to the moors. His Lordship owns an estate up there, with grouse shooting and the like. Dennis Quarmby, one of my patients, is his gamekeeper, and the husband of Gillian, the practice nurse, is his estate manager.' He checked his watch. 'And now I need to be going. I've left Ben Allardyce coping with the late surgery on his own, which is a bit much, but fortunately he doesn't seem to mind. What are *you* going to do now the ceremony is over? Wait for Emma to appear?'

'Yes, I'm expecting her at any moment. She was with those watching and then the photographer approached her. She will know that I'm free now, and then after I've tidied up I think I'll call it a day.'

He was on the point of departure. 'Yes, do that. Have a nice weekend, Lizzie.' Hoping that she might pleasantly surprise him, he added, 'What do you usually do?'

'A big shop on Saturdays and maybe take in a film. On Sundays I do my laundry and tidy up wherever I'm living at the time.'

He wondered what she meant by 'living at the time', but didn't comment. Had she come from a series of bedsits? But he'd asked enough questions. Any more could be seen as intrusive and as it appeared that she wasn't interested in how *he* spent *his* weekends or, if she was, she clearly wasn't going to ask, he said goodbye and returned to his patients.

With Emma sitting opposite her, Lizzie was discovering that she was thirty-two years old and, according to the date of her last period, was now eight weeks pregnant.

'Your blood pressure is fine,' she told her when she'd checked it, 'but I see from your notes that you're on medication for it, so we'll keep a close eye on that.' She gave her a reassuring smile. 'How are you feeling?'

'I've got morning sickness and sore breasts so far,' Emma told her.

'Both to be expected, I'm afraid. For the morning sickness try smaller meals more frequently, and ginger biscuits or ginger tea will help lessen the nausea. What about tiredness and exhaustion?'

'Oh, I'm tired all right, and it's partly due to the tea rooms being so busy, as well as my being pregnant. Simon wants me to take a back seat and employ someone to take my place, but I don't know that I want to sit around all day.'

'Perhaps a bit of both is the answer,' Lizzie suggested. She gave Emma a pregnancy pack full of information, took bloods and a urine sample, and arranged the twelve- and twenty-week scan dates. 'I'll see you in a month's time, Emma, unless you have any concerns before then.'

About to lock up, she looked around her and thought that it was just a week since she'd arrived in Willowmere and it had been a strange one. Since meeting James Bartlett at the wedding and then again with his children outside the Hollyhocks Tea Rooms, he'd seemed to be everywhere she'd turned, though she'd been the one who'd kick-started the cow episode that she would so much like to forget.

He had asked how she usually spent her weekends and she'd told him without embellishments, as she didn't see it being any different here in Willowmere, except that she might get out more on foot than she'd done in the town as the countryside was breathtaking.

She went to bed early but sleep was a long time coming because her mind was full of the day's events: the exciting opening of the clinic; the unexpected offer of help from Olivia Derringham; Emma's pregnancy after a long time of waiting; and in the midst of it all was the amazing James with his busy, well-organised life, which included the enormous task of bringing up his children on his own.

No matter how much help he had from outside, the responsibility for their health and happiness was his, and having met the delightful pair briefly it would seem that he was to be congratulated.

She would have done the same if she'd been given the chance, she thought as she twisted and turned under the covers, but it hadn't worked out like that, and ever since she'd been living in a cold zone with regard to family life.

As the hours ticked by, sleep was coming at last. Soon she would slide into oblivion's comforting respite, she thought drowsily, but it was not to be. The bedside phone was trilling and when she picked it up James's voice came over the line.

'Lizzie,' he said, 'I'm sorry about this.'

'It's all right,' she told him, unable to disguise her surprise. 'What is it, James?'

'We have a pregnant patient who has got a bleed. They've been in touch with the emergency services but there is going to be some delay as there has been a serious accident on the motorway and there are huge hold-ups, so I'm going up there to check her out. She lives in a remote farm on the edge of the moors and the thing is, she's asking for you.'

'Is she one of those whose notes you've passed on to me?' she asked, now fully awake.

'No, she's from your St Gabriel's clinic and was about to transfer to Willowmere when she heard you were going to be based here, but this has cropped up. Can I ask you to come with me? I know that it's barely seven o'clock, but her mother says she's frightened and very weepy.'

'Of course I'll come. Who is she, James?'

'Kirsten Williams. Do you recall her?'

'Yes. She's seventeen years old and due to give birth in a couple of months. I've been seeing her regularly at the hospital. Kirsten didn't want to have the baby at home and has had no problems so far. This is something out of the blue.'

'It would seem so,' he agreed. 'Is it too soon to say I'll pick you up in ten minutes?'

'No. I'll see you then.'

She was at the gate waiting for him, dressed in her uniform, devoid of make-up and with hair tied back loosely. There had been no time for the long fair plait that he was getting used to seeing.

As she settled herself in the passenger seat he said, 'Having to forego your breakfast is getting to be a habit, isn't it? I really am sorry to be having you back on the job so soon.'

She smiled across at him. 'Today it is for a much more worthy cause, and what about *your* breakfast? I presume Helen will be giving the children theirs?'

'I've already seen to that,' he said with a wry smile, 'and, yes, she's with them now. I asked her if she could pop round to keep an eye on them as she doesn't usually come to us at the weekend. Their day starts quite soon, I'm afraid. Children who go to bed early get up early.'

'Yes, I would imagine so,' she said, and there was something in her tone that told him to drop the subject.

As he drove up the hill road she said, 'I'm going to have to get to know the area and have bought a couple of maps but they're in my car, and even so, if I'd been on my own I would have been floundering a bit.'

He was pulling up outside a rambling farmhouse and almost before they'd got out of the car Kirsten's mother was framed in the doorway and in a nearby field a man waved in their direction and carried on baling hay.

There was no sign of an ambulance so it seemed that the motorway was still blocked and James said in a low voice, 'If she needs to go to hospital we might have to take her, Lizzie, and we'll have to use the side roads instead.' She nodded. The thought had already occurred to her and she smiled reassuringly at the anxious mother, who had led the way upstairs the moment they'd set foot in the house.

'Lizzie!' the girl on the bed wailed when they entered a bedroom so much that of a teenager it made what they were there for seem bizarre, but it wasn't the first time they'd been in that sort of situation and it wouldn't be the last.

As James examined Kirsten she sobbed. 'If I lose the baby it will be my fault because I've said all along that I didn't want it, that I was going to have it adopted, but I didn't really mean it. I want my baby, Lizzie!'

'It's OK, Kirsten,' she said gently, taking hold of her hand. 'We're here and if Dr Bartlett decides you need to go to St Gabriel's and the ambulance still hasn't arrived, we'll take you. Are you hurting anywhere?' she asked with the thought of a slow labour in mind, or even a faster one.

Kirsten shook her head. 'No. It's just the blood.'

'When did it start?'

'It was there when I got up to go to the bathroom early this morning.'

'How much?'

'More than spotting, and it was bright red.'

James had finished examining her and, observing Kirsten's mother, white-faced and anxious, said, 'Kirsten will be better off in hospital, Mrs Williams, and we can check the baby there.' He turned to the girl on the bed. 'You haven't had any falls or accidents in the last few days?'

'No, nothing.'

'Pregnant women do sometimes experience blood loss during pregnancy,' he explained, 'so we're going to take you to hospital and place you in their care.'

'I've got a case packed,' her mother said, 'and I'm coming with you. I would have taken Kirsten myself but I don't drive, and the farmhand is too busy to leave what he's doing.'

Was there no husband and father in this household? Lizzie wondered. There'd been no mention of one. Perhaps Mrs. Williams ran the farm single-handed except for the man they'd seen baling the hay.

Having taken note of her mother's comments, James was turning to Kirsten and saying, 'Just slip on a robe of some sort, Kirsten, and once we've got you and your mother settled in the back seat of the car with a blanket round you, Lizzie and I will take you to St Gabriel's by a different route from the one that's blocked.'

While he'd been speaking Lizzie had cancelled the call to the emergency services and within minutes they were off, driving through the still sleeping village in the quiet morning.

As the buildings of the big hospital in the nearest town came into sight Lizzie was thinking that this was unreal. She'd been gone from St Gabriel's for just one week and she was on her way back to the wards that she knew like the back of her hand, and driving them there was the man that she'd thought would be just a figurehead at the surgery, someone that she saw briefly during working hours.

Instead, it was as if he was taking over her life with his brisk concern for his patients and her own well-being, and though it was very pleasant in one sense, there was the risk that she could get to like it, which just wouldn't do. The last thing she would ever want would be to make a fool of herself over James Bartlett.

In everything except her innermost feelings she was cool and capable but relationships of a personal kind were taboo. So why would she be there like a shot if James invited her out again? He was someone dedicated to looking after others, she thought, even putting up with an outsider who didn't know her own mind.

* * *

'Lizzie! What are you doing here? Dare I hope that you've come back to us?' Giles Meredith, the top gynaecologist at St Gabriel's, said in greeting when he came to see Kirsten in the emergency admissions section of the maternity wing.

He shook hands with James and said, 'It must be some service you are giving your pregnant patients if both their GP and midwife are bringing them here in person.'

Lizzie smiled, the two of them went back a long way. Giles was the nearest thing to a father figure she'd ever known as she'd lost her parents when quite young and been brought up by her mother's unmarried sister, who had endured the responsibility for just as long as was necessary and then been eager to take a back seat.

'Maybe you haven't heard that the motorway is blocked, Giles,' she explained. 'The emergency services couldn't get through to us and we needed to bring Kirsten here as quickly as we could.'

James sensed an easiness in Lizzie's manner towards the well-respected Giles Meredith that he hadn't witnessed before, and again he wondered which was the real her, the restrained loner, or the bright, career-minded midwife. Or maybe there was yet another side to Lizzie that he had yet to see.

'Ah, I see,' the gynaecologist commented, and he turned to where Kirsten was lying hunched on the bed in a small cubicle with her mother seated beside her. 'It says on your admission notes that you've had some bleeding, Kirsten. Is that right?'

She nodded mutely.

'In that case, an ultrasound scan is called for.' She observed him in alarm and he was quick to reassure her. 'We just need to see how baby is doing. We will be keeping you in for the time being until we are confident all is well, but before you have the scan I want to examine you. Again, it won't hurt. Then we'll see what your blood pressure has to tell us.'

'We are going to leave you with Dr Meredith now, Kirsten,' Lizzie told her. Turning to her mother, she said, 'He is the best, Mrs Williams. Kirsten will be in safe hands.'

'So you're not coming back to St Gabriel's, then, Lizzie?' Giles teased as they prepared to leave.

'No,' she replied, 'and if you saw Willowmere and the new clinic you would understand why.'

And what about the handsome widower by your side, doesn't he have anything to do with it? he thought, but Lizzie was Lizzie and since she'd lost her husband she'd never shown interest in anyone else.

As they were about to pull out of the hospital car park a few minutes later James said, 'What is your guess about the bleeding?'

'Placenta praevia? The placenta is too low and blocking the uterus?'

'Hmm, great minds think alike. We'll have to see what Meredith comes up with, though.'

'Yes, of course. I've just told Kirsten's mother that he is the best. Giles is a friend as well as a colleague. He was there for me at a very bad time in my life.'

There was silence as James waited for her to continue

satisfying his curiosity, but it seemed as if that was to be his crumb for today and he didn't pursue it.

Yet it seemed that there was another little snippet of information coming his way from the woman who had appeared in his life and was making the road he was used to travelling seem rigid and unexciting.

Lizzie was pointing to a block of apartments opposite the hospital. 'You see the one with the 'For Sale' sign? It's mine. That's why I'm renting the cottage near the peace garden. I can't buy a place in Willowmere until it's sold.'

'I see,' he said slowly. 'So you were even nearer the job here than you are now. Did you never find it rather suffocating?'

'Occasionally maybe, but I needed somewhere to live and it was convenient.'

'Do you want to go across to check that everything is secure? There might be some mail.'

'I rarely get mail,' she told him evenly, 'but, yes, I suppose I could while I'm here, though I've only been gone a week. Do you want to come with me, or wait in the car?'

There was only one answer to that, James thought. His curiosity wasn't going to let him stay where he was, though he couldn't see an empty apartment providing any clues about Lizzie's life before Willowmere.

'I'll come with you,' he replied.

As he stepped over the threshold he saw immediately that it was a modern, soulless sort of place, the kind where one could go weeks without seeing another resident. But maybe after a long hectic day on the maternity wards it was what Lizzie had felt she needed.

Everything was intact, and as she'd thought there was no mail. As if reading his mind, she said, 'It's a far cry from where I'm living now, isn't it?'

He could hardly disagree with that. 'Yes, I suppose it is, and if it is solitude you want you won't get much of that in Willowmere where we all look out for each other.' Unable to resist the opportunity, he asked, 'But why, Lizzie? What has life done to you to make you feel like that?'

It was a beautiful day but her smile was wintry as she told him, 'I'll tell you some time, and hope that you of all people will understand, but at the moment I'm starving. Can I treat you to breakfast somewhere?'

I'm all for stopping to eat,' he agreed, taking the hint, 'but if you want to be independent, how about fifty-fifty?'

'No. You had Helen feed me the other day if you remember, so now it's my turn.'

Her manner was more relaxed now and he thought that Lizzie would be even more beautiful with the long fair plait, expressive eyes and fine-boned slenderness if she was cherished and content instead of the solitary woman that she seemed to be. But maybe she preferred her completely independent life.

'Is there a Mr Williams?' she asked as they drove around, looking for somewhere to eat. 'I got the impression without anyone actually saying so that there wasn't.'

He nodded. 'You could be right. I've not been called out to the farm often over the years, and when I have been I've only ever seen Loretta Williams and Kirsten there, as if the mother runs the place herself. There's no Mr Williams registered with us. But it's isolated up there. If that is the case one would expect Loretta to be able to drive, unless the fellow who waved to us has a car and lives in.'

Unaware that just a few moments ago James had been taking stock of her, while they'd been discussing the absent husband Lizzie had been thinking that his eyes were so amazingly blue the tiny creases round them were barely visible, and though he had a strong jaw line, his mouth was kind, and when she saw that he was observing her questioningly she said to change the subject, 'Were the children still asleep when you phoned me about Kirsten?'

'No, as I left Helen was giving them their breakfast. When they heard me say I would pick you up they wanted to come with me, which they couldn't, of course, so to take their minds off it I promised to let them stay up late tonight.

'They're a handful sometimes, but they're good kids. Polly is the easy one to cope with, what you see is what you get with my small daughter, but Jolly is a different matter and doesn't always live up to his name. Yet they get on well together in spite of the difference in their personalities.'

He found a parking space and pulled in. 'They have no mother as Jolly was quick to inform you when we met outside the Hollyhocks on the day of Laurel and David's wedding, but as well as having me there all the time they have Jess and Helen, and my sister, Anna, who will shortly be coming home from Africa, adores them, and that being so we do the best we can. Right, this isn't appeasing our hunger, is it? Shall we go and find the nearest eating place that is serving breakfast?'

As they ate together in a café in the town centre Lizzie was experiencing a feeling of unreality. It was as if the clinic was something in the background and the man seated opposite was the reason why she'd come to Willowmere, which was crazy.

She needed Monday morning to come quickly, she thought, so that the job she loved would fill her thoughts instead of the village doctor that she was seeing so much more of than she'd expected. Her career had been her lifeline over the last three years and she wanted it to stay that way.

James was just part of the package, she told herself, but when she looked up from the cooked breakfast she'd ordered to find him observing her thoughtfully she could feel her face warming.

'What?' she asked uneasily.

He smiled. 'I was thinking that you might be feeling that I'm crowding you a bit, that you haven't come up for air since you came to the village. Lizzie, did you have any regrets while we were at St Gabriel's with the chance to compare the two? It registered that Giles Meredith would like to have you back.'

'That was just Giles,' she said, regaining her composure, 'and you heard what I said to him, didn't you? That if he saw the village and the clinic he would know there was no chance.'

She wasn't to know that Giles would have put the man sitting opposite at the top of her list of reasons for liking the place if he'd been asked.

Her response to James's first question was slower and she sensed he guessed what was going through her mind. 'No, I don't feel overwhelmed by you, certainly not with regard to the job,' she told him, 'but I've been out of circulation in every other way for quite some time, my own choice by the way, and am not sure how much I want to have to polish up my social graces to get back into it.'

It was only half the story, she thought sombrely, but she wasn't going to open up her heart to a man she'd only just met, even if he was as kind and charismatic as this one.

His brow was clearing. 'That's all right, then. Just as long as I'm not crowding your space. By the way, when the children heard me on the phone to you this morning Polly said, "Is it the lady with the blue shoes?" I can see that you will have to keep your eye on them or she'll be asking if she can add them to her collection.'

'I'd already decided to give them to her as they aren't very comfortable,' she told him. 'Yet I can't do that without finding something for Jolyon too. As soon as I do, she can have them.'

'I can't let you do that!' he exclaimed. 'If I remember rightly, they looked expensive and I don't want Polly to think she can coax them off you.'

Lizzie felt her cheeks start to warm again. There

must be those of her sex who would like to take the reluctant widower to the altar and saw his children as a means of getting him there.

She shuddered to think that he might suspect that the newcomer to Willowmere came into that category, and her calling him out to the bull that had been a cow came to mind.

James had already finished eating and when she pushed her plate to one side, having suddenly lost her appetite, he said, 'Are we ready to go, then? Helen said there was no need for me to rush back, but I don't want to be too long as she looks forward to her weekends.'

'Yes,' she said, getting to her feet, and went to pay for the food before he could intervene.

There was silence between them on the journey back to Willowmere, with Lizzie feeling that the least said the soonest mended, and James wondering why what he'd said about Pollyanna and the shoes should create coolness between them. The last thing he wanted was for Lizzie to feel that she had to bring gifts for his children.

CHAPTER FOUR

WHEN they arrived back in Willowmere James stopped the car in front of Bracken House and said, 'I'll let Helen know I'm back before I drop you off at your place.'

At the same second that he got out of the car the front door opened and Pollyanna and Jolyon came running down the path, crying excitedly, 'Daddy! Are we going to the park?'

Lizzie felt envy rise in her throat like bile. If only her baby had been spared, she thought, holding back tears. It would have given some sort of purpose to her life.

When James went to greet them he held out his arms, and as they ran into the circle of them she turned away, surprised at the wave of emotion that such a simple gesture had caused.

When she turned back the three of them were approaching, and she swung her legs out of the car and stood waiting for them to draw level, ashamed at being envious of the life James had made for himself and his children. She dredged up a smile.

He was some man, this country doctor, she thought.

He had to be for him to be making such an impression on someone like herself, who had jaundiced views on almost everything except maternity care.

It couldn't be easy with a busy practice to run, as well as bringing his children up on his own in a stable family home, and with no one to turn to for comfort in the dark hours of the night. But it seemed as if that was the life he had chosen for himself and he seemed content enough.

The children were observing her curiously, Pollyanna smiling and bright-eyed and Jolyon with a youthful gravity that made her want to sweep him up into her arms and kiss away his frowns.

'We always go to the country park by the river on Saturday mornings,' James explained into the silence that had fallen upon them. 'There is a safe children's play area, a pond covered in waterlilies, where the heron rules the roost, and lots of wildlife all over the place that are attracted by the river.'

'We take bread for the ducks as well,' Pollyanna explained.

'Mmm! It sounds like great fun,' Lizzie told her, suitably impressed. 'I'll have to go and see the park for myself one day.' She looked at James. 'So why don't you go now? There is no need to drop me off at the cottage—it's only minutes away.'

'If you come with us you can see the ducks and the swings and everything now,' Pollyanna said, her quicksilver mind leaping ahead.

'Lizzie might have other things to do, Polly,' James said in mild reproof.

'If I have, they can wait,' Lizzie said, smiling down onto the little girl's upturned face, unable to resist. 'That would be lovely, as long as *you* don't mind me tagging along, James.'

'Of course not,' he said easily. 'It will be someone to chat to while the children feed the ducks and play on the swings. I'll just pop inside to thank Helen for holding the fort and wish her a pleasant rest of the weekend, and then we'll be off.'

As soon as she'd agreed to join them Lizzie wished she hadn't, but she couldn't resist Pollyanna's suggestion and when it seemed as if James had no problem with her joining them the idea had taken hold of her. But now as they approached the park beneath a mellow sun she wasn't so sure. She was going to be butting in on one of the children's weekend treats and James would have invited her along out of politeness.

Yet those doubts were soon laid to rest when they arrived at the play area of the park. Pollyanna was up the steps to the top of the slide within seconds, but Jolyon stood watching, instead of following his sister.

James had gone to catch her at the other end and the cautious member of the twosome asked, 'Will *you* come down the slide with me, please?'

'Oh…yes, of course I will,' Lizzie told him, the urge to hold him close coming over her again. 'If you get on first, I'll sit behind you and hold you tight.'

When James looked up after catching Pollyanna at the bottom and saw them coming down, his eyes widened, and before he could say anything Jolyon was pulling on Lizzie's hand the moment they were back on their feet and crying, 'Again!'

'Incredible!' his father in a low voice as his son raced back up the steps. 'I can't count the number of times I've tried to get Jolly to come down the slide with me when he didn't want to come down on his own, but he's such a cautious child.' His glance took in Lizzie's slender-ness. 'He was always afraid I would get stuck between the two sides.'

'Lady!' Jolyon was shouting from the platform up above, and James frowned.

'You'll have to excuse him, but he doesn't know your name, does he? What do you suggest the children call you?'

'Just Lizzie. I don't mind.'

'Are you sure?' he called as she began to climb the steps.

'Yes, I'm sure,' she replied, smiling down at him.

The two of them had been down the slide at least a dozen times and now Jolyon was sliding down on his own, and as James came striding across from where he'd been pushing Pollyanna on the swings he said laugh-ingly, 'There's an ice-cream van over there. Can I buy you a cornet as a token of my appreciation for the way you've helped Jolly to conquer his fears?'

Her eyes were sparkling, her mouth tender, and he thought that she was beautiful when she was happy, and happy Lizzie had been while they'd played with the children. She would make some child a lovely mother, but was there a man in her life?

There was no sign so far, despite the wedding ring. He supposed he could sound Giles Meredith out about it, but he wouldn't do that. It would be an invasion of her privacy and there was nothing to say that Giles would be willing to satisfy his curiosity if he did.

They'd fed the ducks that had been out of the water and on the river bank in a flash when the children began to throw the bread. Had watched the heron bend its long neck before dipping its beak in the lily pond and coming up with a flapping fish, and now it was time to go.

The children were hot and hungry, ready for their lunch, and Lizzie was starting to feel as if she'd been around long enough as a result of Pollyanna's impulsive invitation. For all she knew, James might be putting up with her company on sufferance just to please the children.

As she was about to say goodbye Jolyon's solemn blue gaze fixed on her and he said, 'Will you come and play with us again?'

Before she could reply Pollyanna enquired, 'Have *you* got any boys and girls?' And now it was James who seemed to be watching her intently.

'No. I haven't got any children,' she told her, 'and, yes, I'd love to play with you both again, Jolyon, but it will depend on what your daddy says. My name is Lizzie, by the way, and I'm a nurse, the kind that helps babies to be born.'

She sent James a smile. 'I don't want to intrude in your lives. I'm going, James. I'll see you on Monday with flags flying and doors open at the new centre. All I need now are some patients.'

'They'll be there,' he promised, 'enough to keep you fully occupied. You might be glad of some help from Lady D. Enjoy what's left of the weekend, Lizzie.'

'We'd like a baby to love, wouldn't we, Jolly?' Pollyanna said, halting Lizzie in her tracks. 'Could you get *us* one? But you need a mummy for a baby, don't you, and we haven't got one.'

'That might be a bit difficult, then. I think that you'd better talk to your daddy about it,' she told her gently, and she glanced at James, who was observing his daughter with raised brows. 'Over to you, Dr Bartlett.'

As she let herself into the cottage Lizzie was smiling, even though she knew she was doing the very thing she'd always vowed not to, but how could she resist those children? They were so different, so enchanting, but she had a feeling that the pleasure of spending time with them would be short-lived.

There must have been lots of willing members of her own sex eager to be a second mother to them and a new wife to their father, but it was clear that like herself James had no inclinations of that sort. So she couldn't see an invitation to go to the park with them being repeated, and in any case it had been Pollyanna's idea, not his. He'd gone along with it because his small daughter had put him on the spot.

She spent the rest of the weekend washing, ironing and unpacking her belongings, and on Sunday morning rang St Gabriel's to check on Kirsten. They confirmed that it was placenta praevia that was causing the bleeding. That was the bad news. The good news was that it had stopped and the placenta was almost back where it should be, but they had no intention of sending her home until they were satisfied there was no danger to mother or baby.

Lizzie wasn't going to disagree with that. For one thing Kirsten had been her patient previously and might soon be again if she transferred to the new clinic, and she had all the sympathy in the world for young girls who were left to cope alone with the results of teenage hormones.

Every time she thought about Pollyanna asking her to get them a baby James's expression came to mind, and she had to smile. She was bright, didn't miss a thing, and at almost six years old was just as aware as Jolyon in his deeper-thinking way that the usual procedure for having a baby required a mother.

When it had come to Pollyanna explaining that they would have a problem regarding that, it ceased to be amusing and Lizzie felt more like weeping. But the only person who could grant them that wish was James and she wondered what he'd said to them after she'd left.

Whatever it might be it was not her business, and as she went up to bed on Sunday night the only thoughts in her mind were about the days ahead in the maternity centre and the challenge that it was going to be.

As she made her way there on a crisp Monday morning, carrying the bag that always went with her when on the job, Lizzie could feel her heart beating faster, and it wasn't just with anticipation.

Her relationship with James had moved on over the weekend with the unexpected invitation to join him and his children in the park, and she wasn't as cool as she would like to be about meeting up with him again.

She wasn't used to being in that sort of situation and if it hadn't been for his children it wouldn't have occurred, yet she wouldn't have missed it for the world. But from now on she was going to have to adopt a more distant approach to everything that concerned them both, with the exception of the clinic, which came top of her priorities.

As she walked along the main street towards the surgery there were lots of people about, residents on their way to work, deliveries being made to some of the shops before they opened for the day, and children on their way to the village school with whoever was in charge of them.

When she looked across the street Pollyanna and Jolyon were amongst them again, trotting along with Jess. James's small daughter was chattering away to her, but his son, who was gazing around him, saw her and she heard him say, 'There's Lizzie!' Polly and Jess glanced across and the three of them waved enthusiastically.

It was just a small gesture but as she waved back there was a warm feeling inside her, a feeling of belonging, being accepted into the community, a fitting start to her first day as the village midwife.

At the same moment that she was letting herself into

the clinic James came through the door that connected it to the surgery, and she was relieved to see by his manner that this morning he was purely the doctor. The easy-to-get-on-with, doting father of before had been put on hold.

Sarah Martin, the young blonde receptionist, was with him and when he'd formally introduced them he said briskly, 'All good wishes for your first full day, Lizzie. You know where I am if you need me. The staff have a coffee break round about eleven. Sarah will sort out yours and hers, and remember there's the kitchen next door if you want to use it at lunchtime.'

She nodded without meeting his glance, focusing on the demands of the day ahead to take her mind off the degree of pleasure she was experiencing in being near him again. Heaven forbid that she should join the list of those who would like to be the second Mrs Bartlett.

James was observing her keenly and wondering what had happened to the delightful woman who had sat on the grass in the park with the children on either side of her, waiting for him to appear with the ice-cream cornets.

But, of course, Lizzie had her midwife's hat on this morning. If he read her mind correctly she would have only one thought in it, the purpose for which she'd come to Willowmere. And that was just how it should be, but it didn't stop him from experiencing a niggling feeling of disappointment.

When she'd left them on the Saturday morning he'd told the children, 'The babies that Lizzie looks after have already got a mummy to love them, Polly. So I'm afraid she can't give one to us, but one day you might have a baby of your own, and won't that be lovely?'

Thankfully that had sent her thoughts off in another direction and all the way home she'd been thinking of names for it.

There were four mothers with appointments that first morning, each at different stages of their pregnancies and with different questions and concerns. She had seen two of them before when they'd been under her care in Antenatal at St Gabriel's and now because they lived in Willowmere they were taking advantage of the new facilities.

Colette Carter, the first one to be seen, was forty-two years old and the owner of a beauty salon in the village. Previously childless, she and her husband, who had a car sales outlet across the way from the post office, had been less than enthusiastic when she'd found she was pregnant.

They were Willowmere's leading socialites and wanted to stay that way, but today when Colette put in an appearance Lizzie discovered that everything had changed. They'd felt the first flutters of the baby's movements and the realisation had transformed the couple's thinking.

Because of her age and the pregnancy being sixteen weeks along, she was due to go to St Gabriel's soon for an amniocentesis to check for any abnormalities in the foetus she was carrying. After Lizzie had checked her blood pressure and listened to the baby's heartbeat, Colette was anxious to know what was involved in the process.

'Ultrasound scanning is used to show the position of

the baby and the placenta,' Lizzie explained, 'and then a needle with a syringe on the end is inserted through the wall of the uterus so that a small amount of the amniotic fluid that surrounds the baby can be drawn off to check for any abnormalities.'

'And suppose there are some?' Colette questioned nervously. 'What then?'

'You will be told about them and the risks involved to the baby and yourself, and you would need to decide whether to continue with the pregnancy or not.'

Referring to the patient's records, Lizzie said, 'There's no known history of Down's syndrome or other genetic disorders in either of your families, but the test is important for your age group as there is an increased risk in women over thirty-five. It's just a precaution, Colette, so go home and try not to worry.'

Of the other three patients with appointments, two were local women who already had young families so they'd been through it before and knew the routine. One of them was in the early stages of pregnancy so it was just a matter of blood tests, a urine sample and checking her general health and lifestyle. The other one, whose pregnancy was further advanced, was due for a blood test to assess the functioning of the placenta.

The last patient due to be seen hadn't arrived and Lizzie went to ask James if he could shed some light on the absence of Eugenie Cottrell.

He had just finished morning surgery and was about to set off on his home visits when she appeared, framed in the doorway of his consulting room.

'Hi,' he said, smiling across at her. 'How has it gone?'

'Fine, so far,' she told him. 'Except that my last appointment hasn't turned up and I wondered if you'd heard anything from her that might explain it. Does the name Eugenie Cottrell ring a bell?'

He groaned. 'She rang just five minutes ago asking for a home visit. I wasn't aware that she's pregnant and was booked in to see you, or I would have come across to let you know that she's got some sort of severe stomach bug. I have her notes here. As one of Willowmere's more colourful characters Eugenie leads a very full life, with lots of partying and suchlike. She's an artist and lives in a cottage called The Hovel in woods near Willow Lake. There was a drink problem at one time. It's to be hoped that it's sorted if she's pregnant. Do you want to come with me, or wait until she makes another appointment?'

'I'll tag along. From the sound of it this woman might need a watchful eye kept on her. Does the name of her property indicate the state of the place?'

'No, not really, it's just her sense of humour. Eugenie attended the same school as me and was a loose cannon back then.'

He was picking up his car keys and heading for the forecourt of the practice, and when she'd been next door to get her bag and told Sarah where she was off to Lizzie joined him with a feeling that it might have been wiser to have made her own way to this patient's home. But considering that it was in woodland and she didn't yet know the area very well, it had to be the most sensible thing to do.

As they passed the lake, sparkling in the midday sun

beneath the graceful willow trees, the house that David had renovated with loving care for Laurel and himself came into view and Lizzie said, 'When are David and Laurel due back from their honeymoon?'

'This coming weekend,' he replied. 'They will both be back on the job next week, which will give Ben Allardyce a chance to spend more time with Georgina and baby Arran. He and she had a rough time for a few years after their little boy was drowned. The pain and grief of it separated them, instead of bringing them closer together, and they divorced. But that is all behind them now and they are blissfully happy.'

'So that is another tragic instance of losing someone who was loved a lot,' she said tonelessly.

He gave her a quick sideways glance. 'You mean, like me?'

'Er…yes.'

In truth she'd been thinking of both of them, but *her* sorrow was tucked away in a corner of her heart and she didn't want to bring it out for an airing while she was with James.

It was clear that in the Willowmere Health Centre of which her project was part, there were two families who had faced up to loss and were getting on with their lives. So why wasn't she doing the same?

Maybe meeting James and the Allardyces was what she needed to jolt her out of the half-life that she'd been living for the last three years.

He was observing her expression and wished he knew what she was thinking. There had to be a reason for

Lizzie's changes of mood. He sensed that something deep within her was the cause of them and wished he knew what it was, but one thing was for sure, he hadn't known her long enough to ask those kinds of questions.

They were driving through the woods now along the rough track that led to the cottage called The Hovel, and she said, 'Aren't the trees beautiful as the leaves start to turn, James? I just love the colours of autumn.'

'Mmm, me too,' he agreed, and as a red roof appeared with a smoking chimney perched on it he wished they could spend the afternoon getting to know each other better, instead of fulfilling the function that was part of his life's blood.

An unshaven guy with a pleasant face opened the door to them when they arrived and after they'd introduced themselves, said, 'Eugenie's upstairs and she has got *some* bellyache.'

'Lead the way, then,' James suggested, and the two of them followed him up a narrow winding stairway into a colourful bedroom with purple satin sheets.

The woman they'd come to see was huddled beneath them, moaning softly, and when she saw them she said, 'I've got the most awful stomach pains, James.'

'Have you been vomiting?' he asked, as he and Lizzie stationed themselves on either side of the bed.

'No, it's not that kind of thing, I don't feel sick, but I've got dreadful pains in my stomach.'

'Are you losing blood?'

'Um…a bit,' she said evasively.

'I've Lizzie Carmichael with me,' he told her. 'She

is the midwife you would have seen if you'd been well enough to keep your appointment this morning. So how long have you been pregnant, Eugenie?'

'I've missed four or five times.'

'And so far you've had no antenatal care?'

'I was feeling OK. It was Zac downstairs who made me make the appointment at the new place in the village.'

'Is he the father?' Lizzie asked.

'Yes.'

'We need to get you to hospital,' James told her after he'd examined her. 'You could be on the point of miscarrying, and that is the cause of the pains. How long have you been losing blood?'

'Since the middle of the night.'

'I've called an ambulance,' Lizzie said decisively. 'The sooner we get you to St Gabriel's the better, Eugenie. I just wish you'd come to us when you knew you were pregnant rather than putting yourself and the baby at risk this way.'

'I know I've been stupid,' the woman lying amongst the satin sheets said, 'but I get so engrossed in my painting everything else comes second. Will *you* tell Zac that I might be going to miscarry?' she begged James.

He sighed. 'Yes, if you want me to, but wouldn't you rather tell him yourself?'

'No. He'll be upset. I don't like to see him like that.' She fixed her gaze on Lizzie. 'If they can save my baby, will I still be able to come to the centre in the village?'

'Yes, of course,' she said reassuringly, 'but first we have to get you into hospital care.'

The ambulance had been and gone with Eugenie's

devastated partner beside her, and as Lizzie and James drove back the way they had come through the woods she sighed. 'I hope I wasn't too hard on her.'

He glanced over at her. 'You certainly weren't happy about our patient not having taken advantage of the care provided for pregnant women. Did I detect a personal note creeping in?'

'Are you just asking or telling me off?' she enquired.

'I'm not just asking and neither am I telling you off,' he replied equably. 'Would you like to tell me about it? You don't have to.'

His quiet, nonjudgmental tone crept under Lizzie's defences. 'Yes, I was once pregnant and lost my baby. Not because of any lack of care on my part, or that of the NHS, or because of the tricks that nature plays, but it was due to someone's carelessness, and I've had to live with that ever since.'

'And the baby's father?'

'He isn't around any more.'

'I see.'

'How can you when you don't know anything about me?' she said stiffly.

'I know this much. You are top notch at the job, you like my children and they like you, but at this moment you don't like me much because you think I'm prying into matters that you don't want to discuss.'

He was wrong there, she thought. She liked him a lot. Too much for her own good. But it would pass and so would the edgy moment that had come from her sharpness with the woman back there in the woods.

It was nothing new. She was never envious when she placed a newborn into a loving mother's arms, but she had to admit Eugenie's lack of care and attention had hit a raw spot.

'You're wrong about that,' she said steadily. 'How can I not like you when you've been so kind to me? Remember the cow episode, and you asking Helen to make breakfast for me, *and*, top of the list, inviting me to join you in the park.'

'But you don't like me enough to tell me what it is that drags you down sometimes,' he said dryly.

'I've just told you part of it. As for the rest, I've learnt from experience that loving too much, giving one's heart to someone completely, leaves no defences in times of grief and despair. So I steer clear of that sort of thing and find life a lot easier by doing so.'

'I take it this is about the baby you lost?'

'Some of it, yes.' There was no way she could tell him that she too had lost a partner in similar circumstances to him, and that instead of facing up to her loss, as he had done, had secreted it away in her heart where it lay like a stone.

'And now can we talk about something else?' she urged. 'Eugenie's paintings, for instance. They were all over the place, weren't they, and most unusual, like the woman herself. She's very talented.'

'Mmm, she is,' he agreed. 'I have one in my bedroom that she painted of Julie, my wife. Eugenie did it from memory but it's an incredible likeness.'

There was nothing she could reply to that. All her photographs of Richard were shut away in a drawer because it hurt too much to look at them. That was the difference between them. James was living in the present, and where was she? Somewhere halfway to limbo?

They were back in the village and as he pulled up in front of the practice he said, 'It's lunchtime, Lizzie. Have you anything planned?'

'I've brought a sandwich and am going to make tea to go with it in the surgery kitchen.'

He nodded. 'Good. I'm going to pop back home. I want to phone my sister in Africa and can sometimes get her about this time, so I'll have a bite while I'm there and will see you shortly.'

As they went their separate ways Lizzie thought that her first full morning at the centre had been memorable, to put it mildly. The last thing she'd expected was to be out in the district with James again for a similar reason to the previous occasion, a pregnant patient who might lose her baby.

When she'd brought Eugenie Cottrell's records up to date she phoned St Gabriel's for a second time to ask what was happening with Kirsten.

She was told that the bleeding had stopped and that the placenta, as it sometimes did, had gone back into place, but that they were keeping the pregnant teenager in for a while longer to make sure that there would be no immediate recurrence of the problem, and after those reassurances she went for her lunch.

CHAPTER FIVE

As THE week progressed, the new centre was functioning smoothly. Lizzie was delighted when James accepted Olivia Derringham's offer of assistance for two half-days per week, and was grateful for her input.

Olivia was pleasant and helpful and thrilled that her husband's gift to the village was now established and working. She told Lizzie that when she'd been expecting their last child, Georgina Allardyce, who at that time had been Dr Adams, had come out to her several times for various problems associated with the pregnancy, even though the actual birth was to take place in a private hospital.

'The village practice is dear to our hearts,' she explained. 'And I've been thinking, what about if some time in the future we could offer the mothers who want to have their babies at home a birthing pool, so that they could have the use of it in their own home when the time came, if they so wished? What do you think? Though we are talking about more funding on quite a large scale, so it might have to wait a little while.'

'That would be fantastic!' Lizzie told her. 'Maybe we could start a fund for it. I'm sure that James would be all for it and so would the more forward thinking of our expectant mothers.'

Olivia smiled at her enthusiasm. 'You could try twisting the arm of the primary care trust, and I'll do the same to my husband.'

When Lizzie met James in the kitchen in the lunch-hour he said, 'You look very perky today. What gives?'

Ever since Monday's visit to the house in the woods and the revealing conversation he'd had with her on the way back, they had met only briefly, usually in connection with those who came for antenatal care and were also involved with the surgery.

On one of those occasions he'd told her that Eugenie had been kept in St Gabriel's for bed rest and to get her blood pressure down, which had been sky high, as he'd discovered when he'd examined her at the cottage.

'According to the father-to-be she hasn't miscarried yet, but as we know only too well it doesn't say that she isn't going to,' he'd said with businesslike brevity. 'He seems a really decent guy and if she does carry to full term I can see him in the role of house-husband, caring for the child while she paints.'

It had been a sombre moment, so it was good to see Lizzie now lit up like a light bulb. She'd made clear her attitude on relationships and he'd been asking himself if it had been a warning, a keep-your-distance sort of statement. The only thing that was clear regarding what she'd said was that *she* had no yearnings towards him.

She liked him for his good deeds, he thought wryly, which made him sound a bore, but that was as far as it went, and for someone who was supposed to be the catch of the village it was black comedy at its best.

'Lady Derringham has suggested that we try for a birthing pool some time in the future,' she said. 'What do you think?'

'I think that we are a long way off that sort of thing. We are talking about thousands of pounds. I read of a similar venture at a birth centre somewhere and it cost in the region of thirty-five thousand pounds. We have to learn to walk before we can run, Lizzie. A thousand coffee mornings and bring-and-buy sales wouldn't fetch in that sort of money, though I do understand your enthusiasm. If I don't understand anything else about you, I understand that.' He was being perverse and knew it. The thought of a birthing pool was as dear to his heart as it was to hers and if the opportunity arose, he would welcome it with open arms.

'It was more the primary care trust we were thinking of and Lord Derringham's fondness for the practice,' she said, deflated by his downbeat reaction. 'But I suppose you're right. Olivia and I were letting ourselves get carried away with the idea.' And picking up the mug of tea that she'd just made, she went back to her own domain.

On Friday afternoon Sarah said, 'Did you know that it's the harvest festival on Sunday morning, Lizzie?'

'I've seen a notice about it,' she replied, 'but hadn't really absorbed it as I've been so busy here. What does it involve?'

'It starts with a parade of the farmers driving hay carts and trucks around the village, displaying their produce, followed by farm machinery such as tractors and combine harvesters, and ends up outside the church.

'At the start of the service the farming families walk down the aisle with offerings from their harvests and place them in front of the altar, and when it is over the foodstuffs are taken to a centre that feeds the homeless.'

'I see,' Lizzie said thoughtfully as two things occurred to her. The first was that it was a lovely idea, and the second that James and the children might be there. Contrary to the comments she'd made to him on the way back from Eugenie's cottage, it would bring light into her weekend if they were.

Saturday had dragged by as Saturdays often did, and on Sunday morning Lizzie joined the village folk waiting for the farming community to appear with their various offerings in an assortment of vehicles.

As the procession came trundling along, led by the village's brass band, a small hand was placed in hers and Jolyon said, 'When are you coming to play with us again, Lizzie?'

She turned. James and Pollyanna were behind her, smiling at the surprise on her face, and contentment settled on her like a blessing when James said, 'They haven't forgotten the time you came to the park with us, Lizzie. You're top of the pops.'

'I don't know why,' she said laughingly. 'Your children are irresistible.'

And so are you, he thought in slow wonder, in spite of you being so much on the defensive sometimes. But that wasn't so today. Lizzie was smiling widely as she bent to hear what the children were saying above the noise of the band, and as the long fair plait of her hair swung loosely with the movement he felt the urge to press his lips against the soft skin on the back of her neck.

She straightened up at that moment and caught him off guard she turned to face him, and a tide of colour rose in her cheeks as their glances met.

'Are you going in to the service when the procession is over?' she asked quickly to cover confusion. 'The children are deciding who is going to sit where.'

'Yes. Of course,' he replied. 'We never miss the harvest. This is a farming community mostly and I think that the children need to know where a lot of the food they eat comes from, don't you?'

'Er…yes,' she replied absently, still thrown by what she'd seen in his eyes.

'So let's go in and get settled, then,' he suggested, 'and am I right in thinking that I'm going to be on the end with you in the middle of your fan club?'

'It would seem so,' she said laughingly, and taking the children each by the hand she led the way into the old Norman church that stood only yards from the surgery complex.

As the four of them made their way to the front so that Pollyanna and Jolyon could see what was going on, there were a few surprised glances coming their way as the church was already half-full, and James thought wryly there was no cause for excitement amongst the locals. It wasn't what it looked like.

He was breaking the routine of almost six years by allowing himself to be attracted to the one woman who wasn't interested in him. The only things that made Lizzie sparkle were the job and his children, and he was damned if he was going to use Polly and Jolly as a means of getting through to her.

When the service was over and the church was filled with sacks of grain, vegetables from the fields and fruit from the orchards, he discovered keeping to that vow wasn't going to be easy.

He always took the children to the Hollyhocks for Sunday lunch. He had a regular table booked and today would be no different except for one thing. They wanted Lizzie to join them, wanted her with them. And so did he, but not in the way it was happening, with the impetus coming from Polly and Jolly. He wanted it to have come from her, but knew that wasn't likely.

She was observing him questioningly and said, 'I don't want to intrude, James.'

'You won't,' he said smoothly. 'I have a table booked, so we won't have to queue.'

He was watching her expression and thought she was going to refuse. Even though she was enchanted by the children Lizzie wasn't going to join them. But he was wrong.

After a moment's silence she said, 'Then that would be lovely, James, if you're sure.'

He was sure. Sure she was only coming for the children's sake, and would accept that for the moment if it was what made them happy. It was strange how they'd taken to her just like that, they all had, and as far as Polly and Jolly were concerned it wasn't because they'd been starved of female company after losing their mother.

There had been Anna, his sister, who'd put her life on hold for them, and now they had Jess, who was great, though she did have a life of her own too and was now engaged to a young farmer from the next village.

And then there was his housekeeper, Helen, who was amazing and very fond of them, but he thought that the children must see something in Lizzie that they hadn't already got.

As they walked the short distance to the tea rooms he gave a quick sideways glance to where she was walking along with one child on either side. The children were chatting to her happily and he thought that maybe Lizzie found something in them that *she* needed, too.

His needs didn't seem to come into it, he thought wryly, but he'd put up with that sort of a situation long enough to be able to cope with it. The vacant space in the bed was likely to be there for some time to come.

He wasn't the only one who'd been badly hurt in the past. From what he could gather, Lizzie too had known sorrow. She'd lost a child, which was enough agony for any woman in a lifetime, *and* the father of it was no longer with her to offer comfort, for what reason she hadn't been prepared to say. But she'd made it clear that she wasn't going to risk getting hurt again.

Yet surely she could talk about it to him, of all people.

He'd had to travel along a painful road himself, though for him there'd been Anna and loving friends to support him, but it didn't sound as if it had been like that for Lizzie.

There was a fresh face behind the counter when they went into the Hollyhocks Tea Rooms and Simon introduced her as his sister. When they'd asked about Emma, and James had introduced Lizzie as the new midwife, he said, 'She's resting and is only going to do a couple of hours each day while she's pregnant.'

'You'll look after her, won't you?' he asked Lizzie anxiously. 'We've waited a long time for this. When she was pregnant before, she was unwell all the time and in the end she had a miscarriage.'

'We will be taking great care regarding that and every other problem that might arise,' Lizzie assured him. 'Do feel free to come to the clinic with Emma when she has an appointment. That way you can keep a check on the progress of the pregnancy first hand.'

'Yes, I'll do that,' he promised, his expression lightening, and as they turned away to go to their table she said, 'It's such a shame that everyone can't look forward to the birth with an easy mind.'

'Yes,' he agreed, 'but it would be just too good to be true if such an amazing and complicated thing was always worry free.' He smiled. 'That's what you and I are here for, isn't it, to iron out the creases if we can?'

With his glance on the children, who were already wriggling onto chairs placed around a table for four, he said, 'And in the meantime, shall we satisfy our hunger?'

Pollyanna and Jolyon were each holding a menu and he said laughingly, 'That isn't necessary. They have the same thing every time we come here.'

'And what's that?' she asked, sharing his amusement.

'Chicken and chips, with ice cream for afters.'

'Sounds good. I'll have the same.'

'Are you sure? There's lots to choose from.'

'Yes. That will be fine. What about you?'

'Salad, I'm trying to keep trim.'

Lizzie looked away. She could have told him that to her he *was* trim, with a few other attractions added on for good measure. He was tall, athletic and attractive in a casual sort of way, with the kind of good looks many women would look twice at.

But obviously he hadn't responded or someone would have stepped into his dead wife's shoes before now. Her expression softened at the thought of Pollyanna's love of wearing her mother's shoes. One day she would give her the blue ones that she'd coveted if James had no objections.

She could have stayed with them for ever, but when they'd finished the meal Lizzie rose reluctantly to her feet and with a smile that embraced them all but was mainly directed at James, said, 'I think it is time I gave you some space. It was lovely to share the harvest with you and be invited to lunch, but there are only so many hours in a weekend, James, and I don't want to intrude in too many of them, so I'll say goodbye until Monday morning.'

She saw the children's downcast expressions and putting to one side her intention of keeping it light between them, said, 'Maybe you could come to have lunch with me at my cottage one day. It would be nice to cook for more than one.'

'Ye-es!' Pollyanna and Jolyon chorused, but James merely nodded, which made Lizzie wish she hadn't been so premature with the invitation. That being so, she didn't linger. She made her way quickly out on to the street and headed for home.

When she'd taken off her jacket and kicked off her shoes she sank down onto the sofa and stared into space, reliving every pleasurable moment that she'd spent with James and his children and trying to ignore the voice of common sense that was whispering in her ear, You're not ready for this.

It was true, she wasn't, but if she looked at it from that angle she never would be. Being with them was chipping away at the ice around her heart and if it began to melt, what then?

Apart from the moment when she'd caught something in his expression as she'd raised her head from listening to what the children had been saying when the band had been playing, James wasn't giving out any signals and neither was she. But it didn't stop him and the children being the first thing she thought of on awakening and the last thing in her mind at night.

For the rest of Sunday she did the few chores needing to be done, and once that was accomplished she wandered restlessly around the cottage's small rooms until the streetlamps began to come on and a yellow harvest moon appeared in the sky.

Slipping on a jacket and picking up her purse, she went out into the night and looked around her, undecided which way to go. She could see the lights of The Pheasant beaming out across the main street and there were a few people strolling in that direction, off to share the company of friends or just simply to relax for a while, and the extent of her loneliness was starkly clear at that moment.

She would stick out as a woman on her own if she went in there, and the last thing she wanted was to be conspicuous. What would James be doing at this moment? she wondered as just a short distance away the lights of Bracken House were lighting up the surgery forecourt. Tucking the children up for the night maybe, or going over the surgery accounts with the practice manager as he sometimes did out of hours.

He wasn't doing either of those things. Pollyanna and Jolyon had been asleep for a while, and his intention of going next door to the surgery to bring back some paperwork that he wanted to look over regarding the practice hadn't materialised because he couldn't concentrate on anything except the effect that Lizzie was having on him.

The way she smiled, the way she would bring herself down to the children's level when they wanted to play, was bewitching, but he couldn't help wishing that sometimes she would elevate herself to the plane that he moved on.

Yet did he want to disrupt the life he'd made for himself and set sail on uncharted seas? He'd put thoughts of Lizzie to the back of his mind when they'd separated after lunch, but Pollyanna hadn't let that last long.

As he'd been brushing her hair before she went to bed she'd asked unexpectedly if she could have it like Lizzie's, and he hadn't been able think of a reason why not, unless it was that for the first time ever he was going to have to make a plait of his daughter's long golden tresses.

He opened the front door with sudden determination. He *would* do some practice work, he decided as he stepped out into another mellow night. No use yearning for what could threaten his ordered life.

As he looked down the street he saw her, standing irresolute not far from The Pheasant, and his intentions to do something useful went by the board.

In a matter of a few strides he was beside her and saying, 'Hello again. Is everything all right?'

It is now, Lizzie thought, but didn't voice it. The pleasure of being near him again was washing over her in a warm tide. 'Yes. I came out for a change of scene and was debating whether I wanted to walk into The Pheasant on my own.'

His smile was wry. 'Can't do anything about that, I'm afraid. I have two sleeping children upstairs, but I can offer you a drink at home if you want to come inside.'

Lizzie hesitated. She couldn't think of anything she would like more but...

'You would prefer it if the children were there, wouldn't you?' he said levelly. 'I'm just a means to you being with them, aren't I? I'm only asking you in for a drink, Lizzie.'

'I know you are,' she replied uncomfortably, 'and I don't need Pollyanna and Jolyon to chaperone us. Yes, I'd like to have a drink with you, James.'

'So come this way, then,' he said calmly, and as they walked the few steps to Bracken House he went on, 'You weren't the only one at a loose end. I couldn't settle and was about to go next door for some paperwork to keep me occupied. You arriving on the scene has given me the excuse I was looking for.'

He led her into the sitting room and when he'd opened a bottle of wine and was pouring it, said, 'You'll never guess what Pollyanna has asked me to do. She wants her hair in a plait like yours.'

'Really!' she exclaimed laughingly. 'I can imagine how much you'll be looking forward to that. I'll bet you wished me far away.'

'Not at all,' he protested. 'With Polly and Jolly having no mother, I'm always ready for them to have the benefit of pleasant and trustworthy female company to help fill the gap.'

'But you've never done anything about filling it yourself…on a permanent basis?'

'I might have done if the right woman had come along, but she hasn't so far and the gap remains. Better no one than make a mistake, don't you think?' With a quizzical smile he added, 'You may be surprised to know that I rarely discuss my private life with anyone. In fact, this is a first.'

Lizzie placed her wineglass carefully on the small table beside her and rose to her feet. She had a feeling like she was drowning. They were discussing the fact that James had no wife. It was a good moment to explain that she had no husband, but the words were sticking in her throat in case he thought that she was using the opportunity to inform him that *she* was available on the marriage market.

'What's wrong?' he wanted to know. 'Why are you about to rush off? Is it something I've said?'

She shook her head. 'No. It is something that *I* have left *unsaid*. You might be surprised to know that my life has not been unlike yours, James, and I can't see it altering in the near future. I was married to someone I loved dearly and lost *him*, as well as the baby I was carrying, in a ghastly accident on the motorway. It was three years ago and I've never found anyone since to equal Richard.'

There was amazed concern on his face and she thought guiltily that the last sentence wasn't true. *She had found someone.* He was standing next to her. And she shuddered to think what he would say if he knew.

'Don't go,' he said gently, his blue gaze full of compassion. She sank back down onto the chair. 'You've had to cope with that all alone? No relatives or friends?'

'There was an aunt way back who brought me up when I lost my parents quite young. But she saw it as a chore more than anything else and was only too willing to let me spread my wings when I was old enough. She hasn't been in contact since, but I do have friends. Giles Meredith at St Gabriel's and his wife were there for me at the time and a few others, but I think they've wearied of my desire for solitude and have drifted away.

'But don't feel sorry for me, James. I have midwifery, the job that I was cut out for, to keep me sane, and I count myself fortunate because now I'm working in this lovely village with you and lots of other kind people around me.'

She was smiling now. 'And if you would like to refill my glass, why don't we drink to Willowmere, the new maternity clinic *and the village practice*?'

As they clinked their glasses together on that he said softly, 'You are welcome here at Bracken House any time, Lizzie. I get weary of my own company sometimes.'

She didn't take him up on that, but as her glance held his over the top of the glass she offered, 'If you have any trouble with the plait I'll be only too pleased to oblige.'

'What? Every morning?'

'Yes, if need be.'

That would suit him just fine, he thought, starting each day with them all together, him, her and the children. But he wasn't going to risk having Lizzie shy away from him by telling her so. Not after them beginning to understand each other better after the revealing conversation they'd just had. So he said with a change of direction but still with the same thought in mind, 'Do you want to go up and have a peep at them?'

'Mmm, yes, please,' she said immediately.

James preceded her up the stairs and led her into a large airy bedroom where Pollyanna and Jolyon's beds were side by side, and as she looked down at them, sweet and defenceless in sleep, Lizzie thought that his children had lots of love in their lives, they didn't need hers.

Unaware of the direction of her thoughts, James said unwittingly, 'Anna will be home soon, as I told you, and they are both really excited as they're very fond of her. For a long time she helped look after them like the mother they'd never known, and I had to be careful who I employed to fill the gap when she married Glenn and went to work in Africa.'

'Fortunately Jess has been great and Helen looks after them like a doting grandma, so the separation hasn't upset them too much. Polly lives every moment as it comes, but Jolly is a different matter. There is a depth to his thinking that amazes me and at the same time worries me. He needs stability even more than Polly.

'I sometimes feel that I'm the only thing in his life that he's sure of and I should have done something about it long ago, but as you've just so rightly said some people are hard to replace, impossible in fact.'

She was one step ahead of him on that, Lizzie thought, by already being in the process of discovering that it wasn't quite so impossible as *she'd* previously thought. She wanted to reach out and hold him close for comfort, but she lacked that sort of confidence and so instead said in a low voice, 'From what I can see, you're doing a wonderful job of bringing up your children, James. Don't ever feel guilty about that.'

At that second Pollyanna stirred in her sleep and he whispered, 'If Polly wakes up and finds you here, she'll be out of bed in a flash, so maybe we'd better go back down.'

She nodded reluctantly and he thought surely Lizzie

could see that he was aware of the attraction she had for the children and that she was equally drawn to them. But he wasn't going along a road that led to a mother for his children who wouldn't love him too, and there were no signs of *that* so far.

It was almost midnight and James wasn't happy when Lizzie got up to go. 'They'll be coming out of the pub about now,' he said. 'It can be a bit rowdy sometimes and I can't leave the children to see you safely home.'

They'd chatted about various things after he'd taken her up to see them, none of them personal after their previous discussion. Then James had insisted that she stay for supper and the time had flown, with Lizzie wistfully thinking that this was what she was short of, some congenial male company. But she reminded herself that the solitary life had been her own choice in those days of pain and grief and she'd never felt the need to regret it…until she'd met James.

'I'll be fine,' she assured him. 'It's only a few minutes' walk away.'

He shook his head. 'That may be. But the fact remains that I invited you here and it's up to me to see that you're safe.'

A lump came up in her throat at his concern and as tears pricked she fought them back lest she make a spectacle of herself. The next moment she was observing him in amazement as he said, 'Helen always keeps the spare room ready in case of visitors. I would be happier if you stayed the night.'

Lizzie could actually feel her jaw dropping. 'And what would I do for nightwear?' she croaked.

'I can find you a pair of my pyjamas. They'll be a bit voluminous on you.' Laughter was in the eyes looking into hers as he added, 'Better too big than too small, don't you think?'

'Err, yes, I suppose so,' she agreed, 'and, yes, I will stay if it puts your mind at rest.' Now it was her turn to be amused. 'But what about your reputation if Helen finds me on the premises when she turns up in the morning, or Jess when she comes to get the children ready for school?'

'Their amazement will only be equalled by their relief.'

'What do you mean by that?'

'At finding me with a member of the opposite sex. I don't know whether you are aware of the fact but the whole village is trying to marry me off.'

'Is that so? Well, I can assure you that I will be long gone before they arrive.'

'OK. Whatever,' he said easily. 'But I will sleep more soundly knowing that you're tucked up in the spare room instead of walking home on your own.'

It was only half-true. He *would* feel happier, but he would also be very much aware that the only woman he'd looked at twice for a long time was sleeping under his roof in a pair of his pyjamas.

When they were about to separate on the landing he said, 'How long is it since you slept with someone else in the house?'

She gave a rueful smile. 'A long time. It will be a

pleasant feeling knowing that I'm not alone, yet I can't complain as it has been my own choice.'

He nodded. 'Sleep well, Lizzie.' Turning, he went into his own room and closed the door firmly behind him as if to say that was the last she would see of him until morning.

CHAPTER SIX

LIZZIE awoke the next morning to the sound of whispering, and when she opened her eyes Pollyanna and
Jolyon were beside the bed in their nightwear, eyes full
of solemn curiosity.

As she smiled at them Jolyon asked, 'Lizzie, why are
you wearing Daddy's pyjamas?'

'They're too big,' Pollyanna pointed out.

'Er, yes, they are a bit,' she agreed. 'Your daddy
invited me to supper last night and it was late when we'd
finished, so he asked me to stay.'

'And didn't you have a nightie?' Pollyanna questioned.

'Not with me, no.'

'You could have had one of Mummy's.'

'I don't think your daddy would have liked that.'

While they'd been speaking Jolyon had wriggled
under the bedclothes and was now snuggled contentedly
beside her. Patting the bed at the other side, Lizzie held
out her arms to Pollyanna and she didn't hesitate.

At that moment James called, 'Children, you are not
to disturb Lizzie. It's Monday morning and Jess will

soon be here. Breakfast is ready so, chop, chop, let's be seeing you at the table.'

Having no response, he was coming up the stairs and as they heard him go into their room the children snuggled out of sight under the bedclothes.

Seconds later he knocked on the door and Lizzie called, 'Come in, James.' When he appeared she asked innocently, 'Can't you find them?'

She watched his mouth curve with amusement as he observed the small mounds on either side of her, and wondered what it would be like to be kissed by him. For his part James was taking in the vision of his unex- pected guest with hair splaying across the pillow minus the plait and the rest of her submerged in his pyjamas.

At that moment the children came whooping out from under the bedclothes with excited cries and he thought that his wish was being granted. The four of them were going to start the day together, but it seemed that the thought was premature as Lizzie was checking the time and saying, 'I need to get mobile or I'll be late for the clinic.'

'Surely you've time to have breakfast with us?'

She shook her head. It was a tempting offer, but she didn't want to be there when Helen and Jess arrived. She needed time to recover her sanity before her working day began, and to do that she needed to be away from James for a while.

Other requirements were that she needed a shower and to get dressed in her uniform when she got back to the cottage. If there was any time left after that she would have some breakfast.

James took the children downstairs and when she was ready to leave, Lizzie stopped in the doorway of the kitchen where they were eating and said, 'Thanks for your hospitality, James, which I would like to return. Will you and the children have lunch with me at my place next Saturday, if you haven't got anything arranged?'

'We don't have anything arranged, do we, children?' he asked the twins.

'No!' they cried enthusiastically.

Just as he'd known she would, Pollyanna asked, 'Can I try your blue shoes on, Lizzie?'

'Yes, of course you can,' she replied, 'and what would *you* like to do when you come to lunch, Jolyon?'

'I want to see Daisy the cow that you thought was a bull.'

'I'm not so sure that Lizzie wants to be reminded of that,' his father said reprovingly.

'I can see that I'm not going to be allowed to forget it,' she said good-humouredly, 'but you can certainly see Daisy if she's anywhere around, Jolyon. For all we know it might be from her that we get our milk.' Her glance switched to James. 'I really must go. I'll see you later at the practice.'

He was at the worktop, pouring that same milk on to the children's cereal, and when he looked up there was regret in his eyes.

'What?' she asked.

'Maybe we'll have breakfast together another time.'

'Er…yes, maybe we will,' she said uncertainly, and wondered what the how, why and where of it would be.

As she left Bracken House, Bryan Timmins was coming up the path with the daily delivery of milk that he made to most of the houses in the village, and if he was surprised to see the new community midwife leaving James Bartlett's house at that time of day, he concealed it well and wished her a civil good morning.

As Lizzie hurried homeward she thought that she should be thankful that it hadn't been Helen or Jess that she'd met back there. That really would have caused raised eyebrows, yet would it have mattered? There wasn't going to be anything between James and herself except mutual respect, and on her part a growing affection for his children that he didn't appear to have any problems with.

He frequently made it clear that he was a one-woman man and until she'd met him she'd felt the same about Richard, but now she was starting to feel that it would be no betrayal of her love for her husband if ever James looked *her* way.

They'd both known sorrow and had kept faith, but suddenly the ice around her heart was melting because she'd met a country doctor who stood out like a star in a dark sky.

He'd said jokingly that the villagers would like to see him take a new wife, but it had been clear that he had no serious intent on that score, and if he ever did have she couldn't see him looking in the direction of someone like herself.

From what she knew of him so far, James would want a wife who would love his children like a mother.

But first and foremost he needed someone who would love *him* as a wife, and when it came to passion she'd only ever made love with Richard and that had been so long ago she'd almost forgotten what sleeping with a man was like. Would her blood ever warm again with the heat that came from desire? she wondered.

They arrived at the practice at the same time, not late but with no time to spare, greeted each other briefly, then went their separate ways. And as Lizzie's day got under way the steady arrival of expectant mothers from Willowmere and the surrounding villages kept her too busy to think about her own concerns.

'Doesn't this kind of job make you feel broody?' Sarah asked when they stopped for lunch.

Lizzie's expression was serene enough, but she admitted, 'Yes, it does sometimes, but it also gives me a great feeling of fulfilment when I've been there for the mother all through the pregnancy and at the end am there to bring the child safely into the world.'

She knew that Sarah was engaged to be married quite soon and said, 'I'll be delighted to do the same for you whenever the time comes.'

It had been said jokingly and Lizzie was surprised to see a warm tide of colour stain Sarah's cheeks. When she spoke the reason for it was there. 'I think it might have come already,' she confessed. 'I've missed two months on the run.'

'And have you done a pregnancy test?'

'No. I don't want to be pregnant before the wedding,' she wailed. 'Sam is in the army and when he came on leave before being posted abroad for three months we got carried away on the night before he left.'

'So why not go to see Ben? He's a famous paediatric surgeon. Not a gynaecologist, of course, but would be a good guy to see if you feel embarrassed about consulting James.'

'I've told James that I think I could be pregnant and he said if I want to consult him to pop into the surgery, though I think I'd rather go to the chemist,' Sarah said. 'But the staff there have known me since I was small and I don't want it all over the village before I've told Sam.'

'So better to see one of the doctors, then, as they are bound by patient confidentiality,' Lizzie soothed. 'They'll be on their rounds now, but pop into the surgery as soon as Ben or James, if you'd prefer to see him, are back. It's a pity that Georgina isn't around. She would be the ideal one to consult, but she's occupied with her own baby at the moment and it could be a long time before she wants to return to the life of the GP.'

The lunch-break was over, there were a couple of women in the waiting room so it was time to get back. Sarah had to put her possible pregnancy out of her mind until one of the doctors came back from his house calls.

When Sarah came back in the middle of the afternoon after going next door, her expression said it all. There was a mixture of dismay and apprehension in it, but there was also a kind of dawning wonder as she said,

'I've seen Dr Allardyce. James had been called out to an emergency and wasn't there. *Oh, Lizzie, I'm pregnant!*'

'So what do you think your fiancé and your parents will say when you tell them?' Lizzie asked.

'Sam will be thrilled. We'd planned the wedding for as soon as he comes on leave once his three months out there are up, and by then I'll be three and a half months pregnant. As for my mum and dad, they'll be a bit stunned at first but as long as I'm happy about it they won't mind. They understand how hard it is for Sam and I to be apart for so long.'

'And are you?'

'Happy? I will be when I've got used to the idea.'

Lizzie was smiling. 'So shall I book you into the clinic?'

'Yes, please,' was the reply, and Sarah went back to her duties with a dazed expression on her face.

'I haven't experienced any morning sickness so far,' she announced when there was a lull between patients in the late afternoon. 'Do you think I will, Lizzie?'

'You might not,' she replied. 'Though you'll be lucky if you don't, but not all pregnant women have to endure it.'

Sarah had gone dashing off home to phone Sam and to tell her parents her news, and Lizzie was on the point of locking up the clinic for the night when James appeared. It was the first time they'd seen each other since arriving that morning, and her spirits lifted.

When she'd gone to the surgery kitchen in the lunch-hour to make a snack he'd been out on his house calls and must have been busy since then as she'd seen nothing of him until now.

She wasn't to know that after the time they'd spent together over the weekend he was feeling the need to be near her again, to see her, speak to her, but not to touch as that could trigger off events that might be regretted in the cold light of common sense.

'So how has *your* day been?' Lizzie asked, taking in every detail of the tall figure in the smart suit, with the direct blue gaze and kissable mouth. Their glances met, his questioning, hers warm, and she hoped he didn't think she only wanted to know him because of his children. In other words, that she saw him as a means to an end. The idea was almost laughable. Wasn't the usual ploy getting to know the children to get to the father?

In truth she was just allowing her starved heart a little ease in the company of all three of them, father, son and daughter, that was all. Yet in that moment in the deserted clinic it was only the two of them that mattered, and Lizzie knew that no matter what she said to herself she was on the point of falling for a man who had kept faith for nearly six years since losing his wife. But was he likely to turn to *her* if he was ready for a new beginning? As her doubts resurfaced, she thought not.

'My day has been a busy one as always,' he said easily in reply to the question. 'Otherwise I might have come across sooner.'

'Did you want me for something?' she asked awkwardly, and he wondered what she would say if he told her that he'd come because he hadn't seen her since the start of their working day and he'd needed to get another glimpse of her before she left for home.

He couldn't believe what was happening to him. The honey-haired midwife with eyes the colour of violets had originally impressed him with her expertise and devotion to the job, but now she was getting to him in a different way and the last thing he wanted was to be out of control of his feelings.

He was sorry for her, deeply so. To lose a husband and an unborn child at the same time was a ghastly thing to have to live with, and from what he'd seen of Lizzie so far it seemed as if it had turned her spirit inwards because *she'd* had no one to turn to.

He had been fortunate in that respect as friends and family, in the form of Anna, had rallied around him un-stintingly and now here he was, nearly six years on and becoming alive again.

She was waiting for a reply to the question and on the spur of the moment he said, 'Helen lives at Bracken House during the week so once Polly and Jolly are asleep I'm free to go out if I want to, and I wondered if you would like to go for a stroll by the lake later this evening, and maybe when the light has gone we could have a drink in The Pheasant or a coffee at the Hollyhocks?'

'Oh, well, yes, that would be nice,' she replied, trying to conceal her surprise. 'What time would you want me to be ready?'

'I'll call for you at half past seven if that's all right.

It should give us an hour or so of daylight before night falls.' Turning towards the connecting door that separated the clinic from the surgery, he said with sudden brevity, 'Bye for now, Lizzie,' and returned to his own part of the premises.

James was already regretting the idea, she thought when he'd gone, and she wasn't so sure it was a good thought either, yet she knew she would be ready and waiting for his ring on the doorbell when half past seven came.

He was late and when she opened the door to him his first words were in the form of an explanation. 'I never leave the house until the children are asleep and they were ages in settling down tonight,' he said apologetically. 'Since learning to read they do the bedtime-story bit and I listen, and the one that Jolly had chosen went on for ever, but they caved in at last and are now in dreamland.'

'You don't have to explain,' she told him gently, her doubts about the wisdom of them being alone together forgotten. 'In any loving family the children must come first by the very fact of them being young and defenceless. Don't ever feel you have to apologise for loving your children, James.'

There was wistfulness in her voice and it made him want to take hold of her and soothe away the pain, but he wasn't going to. He could tell that Lizzie wasn't sure about them spending the evening together, let alone cuddling up to each other, be it innocent or otherwise.

* * *

An autumn sun was getting ready to set by the time they reached the lake and as the house that David had renovated to its former splendour came into view James broke the silence that had fallen between them by saying, 'The newlyweds will be back with us on Monday so we'll be fully staffed at the surgery once more, which will leave Ben free to pursue his own interests if he wishes.'

Lizzie was only half listening. On the day of the wedding she'd been too wrapped up in the bride and bridegroom to take too much note of the house, but now she was gazing entranced at the elegant dwelling that David had resurrected from local stone and carried the name of Water Meetings House.

James was following her glance and said, 'The reason David rebuilt this place was because it had been the childhood home of his mother who had died when he was very young. He had never seen it until he came to live in Willowmere. Just a little further along the road is the place where the two rivers that flow through the village meet, hence the name Water Meetings House.'

'I think I might buy a property when I've adjusted to the new job and new surroundings,' she told him. 'I've been like a piece of flotsam with no fixed abode for the last few years and I'm beginning to feel it is time I put down some roots. I'm committed to renting the cottage for at least six months, but it can take that long for a house sale to go through, so that would be no problem.'

'No, indeed,' he agreed absently.

She observed him questioningly, but it seemed as

if he had no further comment to make so she concluded that her future plans were of no interest to
him, and that she was being a little too hasty in
thinking that his suggestion they spend the evening
together was for any reason other than his desire to
be hospitable.

She might have thought differently if she'd known
that the reason for his reticence was because he'd been
imagining her making Bracken House her permanent
home and had been staggered at the way his thought
processes were working.

But as she didn't, she turned the conversation into
safer channels by asking if he knew that Sarah had
seen Ben that afternoon and he'd confirmed that she
was pregnant.

'Yes,' he said. 'I saw her as she was leaving and she
told me about the baby.' He was smiling. 'Young Sarah
couldn't be in a better place to be pregnant. I'm told that
there will soon be a wedding coming from that direction which will please Edwina Crabtree and her company of bellringers who officiate at all weddings and
funerals in Willowmere.'

They were back in the village and he said, 'So what
is it to be, the pub or the tea rooms…or your place?'

He was sounding her out, she thought. Wary that she
might have her eye on the vacant slot in his life. She told
him coolly, 'I can't see the Hollyhocks being open at
this hour, so perhaps just one drink at The Pheasant and
then I'll say goodnight, if you don't mind.' She didn't
mention her cottage.

'No, not at all.' And where her tone had been cool his was easy as if he wasn't bothered either way.

They had one drink with little to say to each other and James was about to leave her at the gate of the cottage. This was unreal, Lizzie thought as they faced each other in the autumn twilight.

She didn't want him to go, yet neither did she want him to stay, because if he did it would be the beginning of something she couldn't control, and afterwards she would be floundering in all the things she'd avoided so far, such as uncertainty, hope, dismay, all brought about by giving in to the sexual chemistry that was keeping her rooted to the spot instead of bidding him a swift goodnight and hotfooting it inside.

She was about to discover she needn't have got herself in a state. James was turning, ready to go, and saying, 'Some time, if you like the idea, I'll take you along the river bank to where an old water-mill has been turned into a restaurant. That's if you're keen to get to know these parts.'

'Yes, of course I am,' she told him, and asked James if he was offering to play the tour guide out of politeness rather than anything else. 'Why don't we go there next Saturday with Pollyanna and Jolyon after *she* has tried on the blue shoes and *he* has seen where Daisy the cow grazes. It would be more interesting for them than having lunch here, with the rooms being so small.'

'Mmm, we could do that if you like,' he said in the same easy manner, as he took in the message she was giving out. It was clear that Lizzie didn't want to be on her own with him. She'd been edgy all the time they'd been together tonight. Was she afraid that his honourable widower reputation was a front for a guy who didn't miss the chance of a no-strings-attached romp with an available member of the opposite sex when it presented itself?

Thinking that she could at least have invited him in for a drink after giving up his evening for her, she said lamely, 'You could come in for a coffee, James.'

'Thanks, but I need to be off,' he said in a tone that was empty of expression. 'Although Helen is at Bracken House she doesn't like to be kept up too late. I'll see you in the morning, Lizzie. Bye for now.' Then he was gone, striding past the colourful peace garden on his way back to the life that she was envious of in spite of herself.

What had happened? James was thinking. She'd been so cool and reserved and clearly hadn't wanted to invite him in for coffee, though it had fitted in with the rest of her reluctance to be alone with him.

Yet when there'd been just the two of them in the clinic at the end of the day he hadn't been aware of anything like that. There had been a strong feeling of mutual attraction, and if he'd stayed any longer something would have developed between them. But it hadn't been there during the evening and now he was deciding that it must have been wishful thinking on his part.

Olivia Derringham arrived the next morning with some good news that Lizzie was grateful for, after spending most of the night lying awake and wishing she'd acted less like a nervous virgin while she'd been with James. She'd fallen into a restless sleep eventually and had woken up to grey skies and a heavy downpour.

'My husband is meeting the leaders of the primary care trust that controls St Gabriel's next week with regard to a birthing pool,' Olivia said. 'The discussion will be about how much will it cost and how important it is in comparison to other much-needed medical facilities.

'He is going to offer to pay half the cost and that should help to bring about a favourable decision, but he thinks, and so do I, that the trust will want to wait a while to see first how well the clinic works, which could mean some delay. So how does the idea strike you, Lizzie?'

'I think the fact that it is even going to be considered is incredible, and that His Lordship is very generous indeed to offer to help with the funding of it,' she said joyfully. 'I can't wait to tell James!'

'Go and do so now,' Helen said. She glanced at Sarah, who had been looking pensive ever since arriving. 'We'll hold the fort for a while, won't we, Sarah?'

'Mmm, I suppose so,' she said listlessly, and on the point of going through to the surgery Lizzie stopped.

'What's wrong?' she asked. 'Have you told Sam and your parents you're pregnant?'

'Mum and Dad know and they don't have any problem with it, but it's going to be days before I can get in touch with Sam as his troop is out of reach on manoeuvres and likely to be so for some time.'

'Oh, that's a shame,' she sympathised, 'just when you're bursting to tell him your exciting news. *He* might ring *you*, have you thought of that? And you will be able to tell him then, Sarah. Keep your fingers crossed that he will.' Hoping she had offered the young receptionist a little crumb of comfort, she went to find James.

When she appeared in the doorway of his consulting room he observed her in surprise. Gone was the reticent woman of the night before. Her eyes were shining, mouth soft with pleasure, and he wondered what had caused such radiance. He'd like to bet it wasn't the sight of him behind the desk.

'Lord Derringham is going to approach the hospital trust about a birthing pool,' she told him jubilantly. 'Isn't it wonderful?'

'It must be if it can make you look like that,' he said dryly, and watched her delight dwindle.

'What do you mean?' she asked stiffly. 'How would you expect me to look on being told something like that?'

'Exactly as you did a moment ago,' he replied coolly, the feeling strong inside him that Lizzie didn't need a man in her life, she was in love with the job. Which was great, he supposed, and he had no reason to be jealous about that.

But with the feeling of futility that the previous night had left him with he persisted with his downbeat approach to what she'd just told him and said, 'It is good news, but if you remember when the subject came up before, I said we had to learn to walk before we could run.

'It is early days to be thinking of something on that scale, we, and you in particular, have to prove ourselves. The clinic has only been open a couple of weeks and though I have every confidence in you, Lizzie, I'm sure the trust will feel as I do that we need to wait a while.'

'I do realise that,' she said stiffly, 'and so do the Derringhams, but I did at least expect some enthusiasm from you on hearing that it is a possibility. I won't keep you any longer.' And turning on her heel, she left him to his thoughts. They were not happy ones.

What on earth had possessed him to be such a wet blanket? he wondered sombrely. He was as keen on the idea as Lizzie was, probably even more so as he'd long wanted an improvement in Willowmere's maternity services.

But seeing her all lit up about the birthing pool, which would cost an arm and a leg if the idea ever got off the ground, had made him question what it would take for *him* to make her look like that, and he'd been snappy instead of supportive.

He had a patient waiting so couldn't follow her to apologise, but the first chance he got he was going to say he was sorry. What reason he would give for his abrupt manner he didn't know, as he was in no position to tell her the truth in the face of her attitude the night before.

When Lizzie returned to the clinic Olivia asked, 'Well? Was he pleased?'

'I'm not sure,' Lizzie told her with the chill of his manner still on her. 'He seemed preoccupied and also was at great pains to point out that we need to prove our worth first.'

'And what did you say to that?' Olivia enquired.

'That we all know that.'

'James is a great guy and just as keen as any of us to give pregnant women the best service possible. You must have caught him at an awkward moment. He'll be right as rain tomorrow, Lizzie, you'll see.'

'I hope so,' she replied.

It mattered a lot that all should be open between them, and if she'd done something wrong she wanted to put it right. He'd made a quick departure the night before when she'd wriggled out of having him and the children for lunch at the cottage and had suggested that she take them to the restaurant that he'd mentioned beside the water-mill instead.

Maybe that was what had made him so unlike the delightful man she could so easily let herself fall in love with, and that was the crux of the matter. She was out of practice when it came to romance…and family matters, never having had a proper family of her own. She thought wistfully how Pollyanna and Jolyon were completely at ease with her and she with them. If only she could be like that with their father…

CHAPTER SEVEN

LIZZIE was called out to an imminent birth in the lunchhour, leaving one of the practice nurses in charge of the clinic, and as she drove to the market garden on the edge of the village where the Dawson family lived she was hoping that this time it would be a son for Will Dawson and his wife, Melanie.

They already had three daughters and the pregnant mum had told her that if this one wasn't a boy they were giving up. Lizzie had delivered each of the girls for Melanie when she'd been based at St Gabriel's, but on this occasion she was only a short distance away when it was time for the birth...

Melanie was strong and healthy and one of those fortunate women who seemed to find childbirth easy, which was often due to the mother's pelvic measurements, and if everything went to plan she would be up and running soon after the delivery. Putting the washer on and making a meal as if bringing a newborn into the world was all in a day's work.

Sadly, as Lizzie knew from experience, it wasn't like

that with every pregnant woman, and a recent case came to mind where what she'd been expecting to be a straightforward delivery had turned into a nightmare of unexpected haemorrhaging immediately after the birth and had nearly been fatal for the mother.

Fortunately the skill of a surgeon had saved her and Lizzie had seen her recently, looking fit and well with a bonny baby in her arms, but it had been a reminder that there was always the chance of something unforeseen happening in the process of giving birth.

There had been no sign of James as she'd driven off the forecourt of the practice and his car hadn't been there, so she concluded that he was either out on his home visits or having lunch elsewhere, and again she wondered why he'd been so downbeat when she'd mentioned the birthing pool.

Whatever the reason, it had shown her that they were not on each other's wavelengths as much as she'd thought they were, but maybe it was for the best. How often had she told herself that no relationships meant no heartache, and so far it had proved to be true. But that had been before she'd met a country doctor who was every woman's dream man.

It was the same as before when she got to the Dawsons' house. A fast, straightforward delivery for Melanie, but as Lizzie placed the newborn into its mother's arms there was one difference. It was a boy and from the expression on his parents' faces they were delighted that their family was now complete.

'I don't need to initiate you into the dos and don'ts

of breastfeeding, do I, Melanie?' she said with a smile
for the radiant mother when she was ready to depart.
'But I'll be calling each day for a while to make sure all
is well.' And off she went, accepting once again that the
ache that was mixed with the pleasure of every birth she
was involved with was not going to go away.

The afternoon was well gone when Lizzie arrived back
at the clinic, and as soon as she presented herself Sarah
said, 'Dr Bartlett was called away earlier. His little boy
had a nasty fall in the school playground at lunchtime
and he's taken him to St Gabriel's for tests as his head
hit the concrete really hard when he fell. He rang a few
moments ago to ask if you were back and when I said
you weren't he left his mobile number because he wants
a quick word about Jolyon.'

'Oh…right,' she replied, dismayed that Jolyon had
been hurt but surprised that James wanted to speak to
her about it when there was Jess and Helen who would
be just as upset about the accident as she was.

She rang him straight away and when he answered
he said, 'Can I ask a favour, Lizzie, after being such a
pain this morning?'

Yes, of course you can,' she replied levelly, 'and I am
so sorry to hear about Jolyon being hurt.'

'Yes, indeed,' he said tightly. 'He's being checked out
at the moment. There's a large, soft swelling on the side
of his head and one always thinks of a haematoma in
such circumstances.

'The favour I'm asking of you is this. They are going

to keep Jolly in for observation even if the scan shows no bleeding, as it was some fall he had...and he's crying for you.'

'Me?' she questioned blankly.

'It's all about that damned cow. He thinks he's going to miss seeing it if he's still in hospital, and won't be consoled until you are around to reassure him that Daisy will still be there when he comes home...and that so will you, Lizzie. He's fretting about that too. For some reason you have hit the right note with Jolly. I can tell that he's taken to you, that he feels secure around you, which, knowing him, is surprising in so short a time. You'll have to tell *me* where your magic comes from as sometimes even I don't understand him.'

'You are fantastic with both your children, James,' she told him softly. 'I'll come straight away. I've just been involved in a delivery for Melanie Dawson and have no one else booked in until morning, so I'll be with you soon. I take it that you're still in A and E.'

'You take it right,' he said wryly, 'and don't drive too fast. I'll tell him that you're on your way with a message from Daisy.'

Lizzie didn't drive too fast, neither did she drive slowly. There was a warm feeling inside her because James and Jolyon needed her, though she would have wished the circumstances of it to be different. Maybe one day the resilient Pollyanna would also need her, but sufficient unto the day was the wonder thereof.

When she drew back the curtains of a cubicle in A and E, Jolyon was lying on the bed, pale and tear-stained with a large swelling on the side of his head. James was holding his hand and talking to him gently, and when he saw her he said, 'Here's Lizzie come to see you, Jolly.'

'Hello, there, wounded soldier,' she said lightly. 'I've come with a message from Daisy. She says "Moo" and she'll be waiting for you at my back fence when you come home.'

His face broke into a watery smile and she went to sit at the opposite side of the bed and held his other hand. 'So how *is* everything?' she asked guardedly of James, who was grey-faced with anxiety.

'We are waiting to go down to Theatre. Need I say more? he said bleakly, and Lizzie's heart sank.

'So it's as you thought it might be?' she said in a low voice.

'Yes, that's the score. I've just spoken to Ben and he's offered to assist during the operation, and needless to say the neurosurgeon was happy to have someone of his calibre on his team. He's on his way, and with time being of the essence said he'll go straight to Theatre when he gets here.

'Ben lost a child in an accident. His little boy was drowned in a fast-flowing river, so no one knows the agony of losing a child better than he does, and that is not forgetting that you've been through that vale of tears yourself.'

She didn't reply, just nodded and thought that, yes,

she had, but to lose a child that had lived and breathed and had its own special place in one's life must be sorrow beyond compare.

'You aren't going to lose Jolyon,' she said, longing to hold him close and soothe away his fears. 'They will give him back to you safe and sound, you'll see.'

He didn't reply to that, just nodded sombrely and said, 'They're going to have to manage without me at the surgery for the foreseeable future. Fortunately David and Laurel will be back on the job on Monday.' His voice broke and he turned away so that Jolyon wouldn't see his distress.

'I'll stay for as long as you need me,' she told him, still wanting to hold him close, but not knowing what his reaction would be if she did.

He raised his head and their glances met. 'Thanks, Lizzie. It would be great if we are both there when Jolly comes out of the anaesthetic.'

'And we will be,' she assured him.

They walked beside the trolley as the porter wheeled Jolyon down to Theatre, and Lizzie could visualise how much it cost James to step back at the door and hand Jolyon over to those who were waiting there. But he had no choice and as they made their way to a nearby coffee lounge provided for anxious relatives she said, 'Is Helen looking after Pollyanna?'

He nodded sombrely. 'Yes.'

'And what about Jess?'

'She wasn't there when it happened. Jess is getting married soon and has taken the afternoon off to go and

be fitted for her wedding dress. She won't know anything about the accident yet.'

'So are you going to lose her?'

'Maybe. It all depends if she wants to continue. I
imagine she will as they'll need the money like any
young couple starting their married life. Her fiancé is
the son at one of the farms in Willowmere, but there was
talk of him wanting to emigrate at one time. So we'll
just have to wait and see.' Now his tone was grim. 'The
same as we're having to do with Jolyon.'

He sounded so bleak, and before she threw caution
to the winds and did take him in her arms Lizzie said,
'I'll get us a coffee. Would you like a sandwich with it?'

'Whatever,' he said absently. 'I feel as if it would
choke me but I suppose it's the sensible thing to do.'

A nurse appeared beside them at that moment and
said with a reassuring smile, 'Just to let you know that
Dr Allardyce has arrived and the operation is already
under way, Dr Bartlett.'

'Thank you, Nurse,' he said flatly. 'I don't suppose
you can give us any idea how long it's going to take?'

'I'm afraid not,' she told him, 'but as I am sure you
are aware, the usual procedure for a bleed of this kind
is to drain the surplus blood from the skull as quickly
as possible before any brain damage or other dangerous
conditions arise, and once that has been done the patient
usually makes a quick recovery.'

With a sympathetic glance in Lizzie's direction she
said, 'I'm sure that you'll soon have your little one back
with you safely sorted, Mrs Bartlett.'

Lizzie could feeling her colour rising at the other woman's mistake and was about to explain, but James was there before her. 'Lizzie is a colleague at the practice in Willowmere,' he told the nurse and it was at that moment Lizzie knew for certain that she wanted to be more than that to him, much more. But the speed with which James had explained their situation to the nurse made it very clear that he wanted no such misapprehensions to be made about them.

Jolyon was in the children's high dependency unit and had just surfaced from the anaesthetic. When he looked up drowsily and saw them standing side by side, looking down at him, he smiled and asked, 'Am I better now, Daddy?'

'Nearly,' James told him. 'You have to stay here for a little while and then you can go home, Jolly.'

'There *was* a bleed,' Ben had told them after the surgery, 'but not as severe as we'd expected. It's been drained. Jolyon will be a bit fragile for a few weeks so keep your eye on him, James, but apart from that he should be fine. He's come out of it very well and I'm delighted for you.'

'I owe you for this,' James told him huskily, and he shook his head.

'No! Not at all. I wasn't the only one in there.'

Ben glanced across to his neurosurgical colleague, who was asking Lizzie curiously, 'So how do you happen to be involved in all this, Lizzie? Have you left us?'

She was sparkling up at him, joyful at the successful

result of the operation, and watching her James thought enviously that if she was as relaxed and happy in *his* company then *he* might have something to sparkle about.

After those few moments with Jolyon they were asked to let him rest, and as they prepared to go back to where they'd been waiting they saw Jess and Helen, holding Pollyanna tightly by the hand, coming towards them anxiously.

Lizzie stood to one side as James swooped his daughter up into his arms and smothered her with kisses, and then explained the events of the afternoon and evening. As everyone was talking at once she slipped away and once in the corridor moved swiftly towards the car park.

The feeling of being just an onlooker had been strong back there, she was thinking as she set off for home. James and Jolyon would be all right now they had Pollyanna and Jess and Helen with them. The two women had known his children a lot longer than she had and had earned right of place by their sides.

Ben had been getting into his car when she reached the car park and he said with a smile, 'You can head off for home with an easy mind, Lizzie. Jolyon is going to be all right. There was a time when it hurt like hell, using my skills for a sick or injured child when I'd never got the chance to save my own, but since Arran was born all the bitterness has gone.'

'I lost a child that I was carrying in an accident,' she told him, 'and have the same feeling sometimes when I've delivered a mother of her newborn.'

'Ah! So that's the reason for the bruised look that you sometimes have. You may not know it yet, but your work has brought you to a place of healing. I'm not referring to the village practice, I mean Willowmere itself. Give it time, Lizzie, and you will see.

'It has a tranquillity all of its own without being a dead end. It is where Georgina came to heal her broken heart when we lost Jamie and I was impossible to live with, and now that I'm here I'm just as enchanted with it as she is. So don't despair. One day you'll know it is where you're meant to be.'

'I'll try and remember that, Ben,' she said, dredging up a smile.

As they went to their separate cars and followed each other out of the hospital car park Lizzie thought that it all sounded so easy put like that, but Ben was not aware that any healing of *her* sore heart might be a long time coming and she might wish one day that she'd never moved to Willowmere.

When James realised that she'd gone he was aghast… and hurt. Lizzie had been his rock during what had seemed an endless time of waiting, and she'd kept her promise to be there for Jolly when he woke up. So now had she decided that, having done that, she'd done the favour he'd asked of her?

Jolly needed her, and so did he, but it seemed that now Jess and Helen were on the scene, and she'd glimpsed that Pollyanna was all right, she'd gone home to do her own thing without a word of farewell.

She'd reverted back to her other self, he thought, and the caring compassionate woman who was bringing back to mind the long-forgotten joys and blessings of a good marriage had gone back into her shell.

After Jess and Helen had seen Jolyon, and Pollyanna had observed her brother, wide-eyed and tongue-tied for once, James took her and Helen home, leaving Jess to sit with Jolyon until he returned after putting his bewildered daughter to bed.

'Is Jolly going to die, Daddy?' she asked, gazing up at him as he tucked her in.

'No, Polly,' he said gently. 'He's going to be fine.'

'But we won't be able to go to Lizzie's on Saturday, will we?'

'No, maybe not, but there'll always be another time,' he said soothingly, with grave doubts about the likelihood of it.

Lizzie had given him the message stark and clear and it said, *Don't take me too much for granted.*

As he was about to leave the bedroom Pollyanna burst into tears at the sight of Jolyon's empty bed so he picked her up in his arms and carried her into his own room and tucked her into his bed. Within minutes her eyelids were drooping and as he stood looking down at her he thought about how well the children seemed to respond to gentle, motherly Lizzie.

He'd always been aware that by not remarrying he was denying the children a mother's love. But had consoled himself with the thought that better no mother than the wrong one, and now unbelievably the right one had come along. He knew it, but Lizzie didn't.

By the time she arrived back at the cottage Lizzie was dismayed at the way she'd behaved by leaving James without a word, and her mortification increased at the sight of Bryan Timmins and his wife approaching from the peace garden while she was parking her car.

'Do you know anything about young Jolyon being in hospital?' the burly farmer asked. 'It's on the village grapevine but nobody seems to know much about it.'

He was remembering how the new midwife had called on James to save her from the docile Daisy and had sensed that they might be friendly, even though she hadn't been in the village five minutes.

'Yes, I've just come from there,' she told him, longing to get inside and take a long hard look at herself. 'Jolyon fell and hurt his head in the school playground and his father thought there might be bleeding inside the skull.'

'And was there?' the farmer's wife asked anxiously.

'Yes, I'm afraid so,' she told them, 'but it's been dealt with and he is now recovering from surgery. He was due to come here on Saturday and was looking forward to seeing Daisy, and is very disappointed.'

'Young 'uns set great store by some strange things, don't they?' Bryan said laughingly. 'Who'd have thought that seeing that dozy Daisy of mine would have been such an attractive prospect?'

They were about to move on and Lizzie said hesitantly, 'I don't suppose you could…er…'

'What? Take the mountain to Mohammed? I suppose I could. I've transported cows all over the place in me time, but is the young 'un near a window? An' they won't want hoof marks all over the hospital's lawns and flower beds.'

'I know St Gabriel's well,' she said. 'I worked there for a long time. All the children's section is on the perimeter of the building next to a lane that is a public right of way. If you could pull up on there opposite the children's ward they would all be able to see Daisy.'

'All right,' he agreed. 'When?'

'Tomorrow afternoon all right?'

'Yes, as it won't interfere with the milking.'

'I'll check in the morning that it is where Jolyon will be, and if you don't hear anything different that's the plan,' she told him.

'And will you be there?' his wife asked curiously.

'I'm afraid not. I have appointments at the clinic to deal with, but Dr Bartlett will be with him. Don't mention it to him, though, will you? I'd like it to be a surprise.'

She was hoping that it would be more in the form of atonement for the way she'd behaved in the hospital waiting room earlier. Recalling her conversation with Ben in the car park, she wondered just how obvious her uncertainties were to those she met.

James stayed the night at the hospital in a small suite at the end of the children's ward provided especially for the parents of sick children so that they could be near their little ones night and day if they so wished.

He was still upset at the way Lizzie had left so quickly and as he lay wide awake with Jolyon sleeping peacefully not far away, he was admitting to himself how much he'd needed her by his side on one of the worst days of his life. And she'd been there, until Jess and Helen had turned up. For the life of him he didn't get the connection.

But was he ready to admit that he wanted Lizzie on the good days in his life as well as the bad in the form of a binding commitment. Most of the time when they were in each other's company she was on the defensive and he wasn't sure why. Yet there were moments when they were so in tune he felt on top of the world.

Back at the cottage Lizzie rang Helen to ask if she needed any help with Pollyanna, it being the first time the twins had ever been separated, and when James's housekeeper answered the phone she said thankfully, 'You must have read my mind, Lizzie.

'I'm struggling here with Pollyanna. She's breaking her heart because James and Jolyon aren't here. She was fretful earlier because Jolly wasn't there when it was bedtime and eventually he settled her in his room away from the empty bed. But she's awake again and in real distress. If you could come over for a while, I would be most grateful.'

'Of course I will,' she said immediately. 'I'll stay the night if you like. Just give me a moment to find a night-dress and my coat and I'll be right with you.'

'Thanks for that,' Helen said. 'I'm not as young as I used to be for coping with this sort of situation.'

* * *

When she arrived at Bracken House, Lizzie found Pollyanna huddled on the bottom step of the stairs in her nightdress, sobbing quietly, with Helen hovering over her anxiously.

'Hello, Pollyanna,' she said gently. 'Are you missing Jolyon and your daddy? They will soon be home, you know. And until they come would you like *me* to give you a cuddle?'

There was no reply, just a nod and a small hand held out to take hold of hers.

As they walked up the stairs together Pollyanna found her voice and said, 'I was sleeping in Daddy's bed.'

'So why don't I tuck you up in it again?'

'You said we were going to have a cuddle,' was the reply.

'Yes. I know I did.' She opened the small bag she'd brought with her. 'Look, I've brought my nightie. I'll just go and get changed, and we can cuddle up on your daddy's bed if you want to.'

Still subdued, Pollyanna nodded, and when Lizzie returned and pulled back the covers, lay on the bed and held out her arms, the tearful little girl slid into them and curled up against her with a contented sigh.

When Helen came up to check on them some minutes later she found them both fast asleep with Lizzie's arms protectively around Polly, and as she smiled down at them she thought that James must be blind if he couldn't see that the one he'd been waiting for all this time had arrived.

* * *

After checking that Jolyon was all right and had eaten his breakfast the next morning, James went home for a short stay to shower and change his clothes before the neurosurgeon was due to check on his patient.

Jolyon's face was black and blue with the severity of the fall followed by the surgery, and a dressing on his head stood out starkly against the discolouration. But the hospital staff and his father were satisfied with his progress and the young patient himself was gradually getting sufficiently acclimatised to his strange surroundings for James to be absent for a short time.

When he arrived home he found Helen at the cooker and the table set for breakfast but no sign of Polly, and she said, 'She woke up not long after you'd gone last night and was still very upset, but she's asleep now.' As he went bounding up the stairs she was smiling a secret smile.

His glance went straight to the bed when he opened his bedroom door and his heart tightened in his chest. It was true what Helen had said. Polly was still asleep, but she was sleeping peacefully in the crook of Lizzie's arm, with her small fair head resting contentedly against her breast.

Lizzie was awake, watching him with wary violet eyes. Unable to believe his eyes at the scene before him, James thought that while he'd been fretting and fuming at St Gabriel's about imaginary rights and wrongs she'd been there for his children once again.

Lizzie carefully eased her arm from beneath the still sleeping Pollyanna. 'Would you have a spare robe I could borrow?' she asked, feeling a faint flush of colour rise in her cheeks. He nodded and reached into a nearby wardrobe for a silk striped robe that looked as if it was meant for special occasions, and she thought that standing before him in her nightdress surely had to be one of those.

As she took it from him she saw that his glance was on her smooth shoulders and the rise of her breasts under the thin cotton nightgown and it was easy enough to wonder what would have happened if little Pollyanna hadn't been sleeping nearby. But that was why she was in James's bedroom in the first place. There was no other reason she was ever going to be there.

'I was mad at you for disappearing like you did yesterday without a word of explanation,' he said in a low voice as she wrapped the robe around her, 'and then I find that after being there for my son, you have been comforting my daughter. I am truly grateful, Lizzie.'

'Don't be,' she said. 'I've only done what any caring person would do in such a situation and, James, it is I who should be apologising to you for leaving like I did. It was just that I suddenly felt I was taking too much for granted and when Jess and Helen arrived I couldn't see you needing me any more. I wouldn't have left if you'd been alone at the hospital.'

'So that's what you thought,' he said slowly. 'That I was happy to have you around when I had no one else, but once reinforcements arrived you became surplus to requirements. How very selfish that makes me sound.'

'It isn't meant to,' she protested weakly. 'You are the least selfish person I've ever met, and while you're handing out the medals it was just on the off chance that

I phoned to check with Helen that Pollyanna was all right. When she said how upset she was I came straight over. We came up here, had a cuddle and she went to sleep in my arms. She was so upset about Jolyon. How is he this morning?'

'Battered and bruised but chirpy enough. I was close by him during the night and didn't leave the hospital until I'd made sure he'd had some breakfast. He was trying to decide if he wants to be a doctor when I left him.' James checked his watch. 'I'm only here briefly as I want to be there when the neurosurgeon comes to check on him. So let's go down and see what Helen has for breakfast, shall we? Then I'm going to have a quick shower and go back. I intended taking Pollyanna with me, but if she's still asleep when I'm ready to go, I'll ask Helen to bring her later.'

When they went downstairs there was the same good food on offer as on the day when he'd sent her to Bracken House for breakfast after the episode with the cow, and Lizzie held back a smile at the thought of Bryan arriving on the lane with his dairy cow some time during the afternoon while she was working in the clinic.

It was a strange feeling to be having breakfast with James, just the two of them in the big family kitchen, Helen having put out the food and then made a tactful exit. This is how it would be if we lived together, Lizzie thought dreamily, though with just one difference. The children would be there to make it a family breakfast and she would love that, the four of them starting the day together, but she knew that James's thoughts were very different. His mind was on getting back to Jolyon in St Gabriel's as quickly as possible, and who could blame him for that?

CHAPTER EIGHT

LIZZIE wasn't wrong about where James's thoughts were and within minutes he was getting to his feet and saying, 'Ben will be in charge of the surgery in my absence, Lizzie. I'll be staying with Jolly for the rest of the day. I'm keeping Polly off school until her brother comes home in view of her distress last night. I really do appreciate the way you've been there for them both and maybe when life gets back to normal you'll let me thank you in a positive way.'

She gave him a gentle push towards the door. 'Thanks are not necessary, James. Don't worry about this end. I'll be around to assist Helen with Pollyanna if she needs me, and Jess will be here soon, won't she?'

'Yes. She can bring Polly to the hospital later in the day instead of Helen, who could do with a rest.'

'What time will Jess be taking her? Not too late, I hope?'

'Er, no,' he replied, looking puzzled, and Lizzie thought he wasn't to know that the farmyard was coming to St Gabriel's. She was going to ring the ward when he'd gone and tell the nurses to look out for Daisy without James or Jolyon knowing anything about it, and as for Pollyanna, the next time Lizzie went to Bracken House she was going to bring her the blue shoes to play with.

When Lizzie had said goodbye to her last patient of the day it was only half past four and she decided to go straight to the hospital to see James and the children, but first she wanted to ask Ben if he had any messages for James about the practice.

He smiled when the trim figure of the community midwife appeared and when she said, 'I'm off to the hospital to see if there is anything I can do, Ben. Pollyanna was very upset last night at being separated from her brother and I stayed the night with her. She was still asleep when I left this morning and hopefully might be feeling happier, but if she isn't it's a lot for Jess and Helen to cope with while James is absent. I've popped across to see if you have anything you wish me to tell James about the surgery while I'm there.'

He shook his head. 'Only that everything is under control, Lizzie.'

'Good. I'll pass that message on.' She paused in the doorway as she was leaving. 'I want to check on any visitors that Jolyon has had when I get there to find out if one of them had four legs.'

'Four legs?' he said blankly.

'Yes, Daisy the cow is due to visit this afternoon.'

'Right,' he said, adding in the bemused sort of tone

used by those who thought they have a deranged person to deal with, 'I hope she doesn't let him down.' He grinned, unable to resist getting in on the act. 'Will she be bringing flowers or grapes?'

Lizzie hid a smile. 'I'm not sure, but one thing she *will* have brought with her is a full udder.' And off she went with a sense of purpose of the kind that she hadn't experienced in a long time.

She was beginning to belong, she thought as she drove to the hospital between hedgerows dressed in autumn colours of bronze and gold. To be accepted by the village and its people was a warming thought, but to belong to the motherless ones and their father at Bracken House would be heaven on earth.

She didn't think the children would have any problem accepting her in place of the mother they'd never known, but their father was a different matter. She'd thought it before and was thinking it again. If James had coped without the joys of marriage for nearly six years, why would he think of changing that for a dried-up, childless woman whose heart had been frozen for the last three years and was only now beginning to feel warm again?

When she walked into the ward Pollyanna and Jolyon, who was still looking battered and bruised with a bandage round his head, were playing a board game at a table by the window, with James seated nearby.

'And how is my little wounded soldier today?' she asked softly.

The soldier in question didn't reply. Instead, he said

excitedly, 'Lizzie, Daisy came to see me!' He pointed to the lane outside. 'She was just there on the grass with Farmer Timmins!'

'Well!' she exclaimed. 'What a surprise! I wonder who told Daisy that you'd hurt your head.'

When she looked up James was observing her with a quizzical smile and he said, 'I would expect it was someone who is kind and thoughtful and top of the list of people he likes.'

'Is that so?' she replied, not meeting his glance, and went for a swift change of subject. 'So what has the surgeon had to say today?'

'Good progress, he says, and if we promise to see that Jolly doesn't do any chasing around for a while when he gets home, he might discharge him at the weekend and refer him to Outpatients.'

'But can I still sleep with you, Lizzie?' Pollyanna asked, the memory of the cuddles of the previous night still fresh in her mind.

'Well, yes,' Lizzie said hesitantly, 'but don't you think your daddy might want his bed back?'

'I can sleep in Jolly's bed,' James said easily, as if her moving in on a temporary arrangement was no big deal.

'Er, well, yes, then,' she agreed weakly. 'If that is going to make Pollyanna happy.'

It would make *him* happy too, James thought, *and* Jolyon, but he wasn't sure where he, as the children's father, came in her scheme of things. Lizzie's love for Polly and Jolly was plain to see. Would he end up as the hanger-on if he asked her to marry him?

Jolyon had been looking through the window wist-fully when the cow had appeared only feet away, and he'd observed it with high delight, while *his* own first thought had been for Lizzie. She would have thought of this and he could have wept at the wonder of it.

The farmer and the docile Daisy had stayed there for some time, with all the children in the ward and their nurses watching as she munched away contentedly on the grass verge of the lane, and when at last Bryan felt it was time to go he waved goodbye and led his dairy cow back to the vehicle that he'd brought her in.

Her visit had been the main topic of conversation between the children for the rest of the afternoon and as James had listened to them he'd wished that Lizzie could have been there to see their excitement.

He had arranged with Jess that he would take Polly home for her tea and then come back to stay with Jolyon for the night again. The nanny had gone home just before Lizzie had arrived, so now there was just the four of them.

'I'll stay with Jolyon while you take Pollyanna home,' Lizzie said, 'and when you come back I'll go to Bracken House again to spend the night with her.'

James was frowning. 'I can't help feeling that we are putting you to a lot of inconvenience.'

'And what else would I be doing at a time like this except helping in any way I can?' she said coolly, not pleased that he might be thinking that was how she was seeing her involvement in the anxious time that he'd been going through.

And upsetting her further, he said, 'Life has been reasonably free from trauma during the years I've been on my own with the children, but at times like this I feel that they need a mother and maybe it is time I did something about it.

'Anna, my sister, filled the gap for them until not so long ago and they were content. When she married Glenn and went abroad with him I employed Jess and Helen, who are both lovely with the children, but Jess has her own life to lead away from Bracken House and Helen is elderly, which is why I never leave the house in the evening until the children are fast asleep.'

As he was about to explain his true feelings, that, no matter what, he would never marry again if the woman in question didn't love him as much as his children, Lizzie didn't let him finish.

Stung by what she saw as a tactless hint that she might fit the bill with regard to his household arrangements she said dryly, 'So why not try a mail-order bride or speed dating on the internet?'

He flinched, groaning inwardly at what was turning out to be a poor attempt at trying to gauge her feelings for him. His timing had been all wrong for one thing, and giving her the false impression that he only wanted her for the use of, when every time he saw her he was more drawn to everything about her, was catastrophic. He was falling in love with her but so far she'd given no sign that she returned his feelings, and he'd been hoping she would open up to him when he'd explained that marriage was in his mind.

She hadn't finished. 'Maybe we've both kept faith long enough, James, without any means of knowing if our respective partners would want that of us. I'm sure that no one would condemn you if you felt the need to take a fresh look at your life. I might try a little speed dating myself.'

As if, she thought as he stared at her in disbelief. She was already wishing she could take the words back and tell him that she had already met a man like no other, who had gently turned her painful, nightmare thoughts about Richard into just a sad memory, and that now she was ready for a fresh start with him and his beautiful children. But James had just made it clear that he didn't see *her* in that way, and if it had to be as just friends then that was what it would have to be.

He took Pollyanna's hand, kissed Jolyon lightly on his bruised cheek and without any further comment in her direction nodded briefly and departed.

James was back within the hour and found Jolyon having his tea with Lizzie watching over him, and the leaden weight that was his heart became even heavier at the sight.

He'd had time to think on the way back from taking Polly home and had decided that a formal apology without any further explanations or misunderstandings was needed, and was hoping that then they might get back to the no-strings-attached arrangement of before.

On the return journey he'd bought her flowers, a beautiful arrangement of white orchids and pink roses to show how much his apology was meant.

When she got up to go he went out into the corridor with her and said, 'I'll walk you to your car, Lizzie.'

She shrugged slender shoulders inside the uniform that she hadn't had time to change and said with the same coolness as before, 'Please yourself. Why don't you stay with Jolyon?'

His glance went to his son, who was happily munching away. 'He'll be all right for a few moments.'

When they were outside in the car park he turned to her and said, 'I'm sorry for being an insensitive clod before. If you'd let me finish you might have thought better of me.' He took the flowers from the back seat of his car and placed them in her arms. 'I also meant to apologise for being so downbeat about the birthing pool. I think it's great that Lord Derringham is on board and you have my full support, too. Whatever you think of me, I can't manage without you, Lizzie. Can't we at least be friends again?'

She was melting with love for him. How could she ignore his plea? She said softly, 'We'll always be that James, if nothing else. Go back to your son and I'll go and see to your daughter.'

Reaching up, she kissed him lightly on the cheek. Keeping his hands tightly by his sides, he resisted the opportunity to extend the moment into something more meaningful and went back to where Jolyon was waiting for him.

Jolyon was discharged on the Saturday, as had been half promised the first time the surgeon had seen him after the surgery, and when the car pulled up in front of Bracken House with James and his son inside, Pollyanna and Lizzie were waiting at the gate to welcome them.

The last few days had been uneventful, with James at the hospital, Jess taking Pollyanna there later in the day and James bringing her home when Lizzie arrived to be with Jolyon. But now it was going to be as it had been before, with Lizzie at her own place and the three of them in Bracken House, unless something unforeseen happened, and James wasn't looking forward to seeing so little of her from then on.

They were back on amicable terms but keeping their distance and he almost broke that rule when he saw the blue shoes in Pollyanna's bedroom.

He was going round the bedrooms and bathrooms, collecting the laundry after they'd all had lunch together, and he called across the landing to Lizzie, 'You shouldn't have let Polly have the shoes. I can tell they weren't cheap.'

'A promise is a promise,' she told him, the memory surfacing of their brief, angry exchange of words at the hospital a few days back. They had made peace when James had given her the flowers, but it hadn't been the same between them.

There were words unspoken that should be said, she thought wistfully, but neither wanted to hurt the other any more, and so they were communicating, but only on the surface.

Pollyanna was tearful when Lizzie was ready to go home and she said comfortingly, 'When Jolyon is really better, maybe the two of you can come and stay the night at my house if your daddy agrees. Would you like that?'

'Yes,' they chorused. 'Can't he come too?'

'I'm not sure,' she said quickly before James could get a word in, and making a joke of it. 'He is very big and the cottage is very small.'

And that puts me in my place, James thought as he listened to the discussion. *Am I ever going to be forgiven for giving Lizzie the impression that I only see her as a mother figure for my family, when I can't sleep for thinking about what it would be like to make love to her?*

The twins were observing him expectantly as they waited for his reply to what Lizzie had suggested, and as if he wasn't feeling that her cottage wasn't *that* small he said easily, 'Yes, of course you can go. You'll have great fun with Lizzie and I wouldn't say no to some time on my own.' That having been decided, Lizzie picked up her small overnight bag and went home.

Sunday was a nothing day. She did her chores, sat around thinking about James and the way she'd avoided any further closeness with him, and as an early October evening presented itself she turned her thoughts to Monday morning at the clinic.

She expected that Sarah would be in a more cheerful state of mind when she arrived as she'd managed to locate the absent Sam back at base from manoeuvres and he'd been thrilled about the baby after the first shock had worn off. He would be home soon and the wedding arrangements were moving along with speed to avoid his young bride showing signs of the impending event on her great day.

Emma was due for a check-up first thing before the tea rooms opened, and Simon was coming with her as he was keen to be involved every step of the way after their hopes being shattered years ago when she'd miscarried for no apparent reason.

They arrived at the appointed time, Emma looking pale and apprehensive and Simon hovering protectively by her side. Her first words when asked how she was feeling were, 'Awful! I can't keep anything down. I feel so sick all the time.'

Lizzie nodded sympathetically. 'I'm afraid morning sickness affects many women during pregnancy, but it usually lessens as the months go by, Emma. Try eating smaller, more frequent meals, and ginger biscuits and ginger tea help to take the nausea away for some women.'

She had Emma's file opened in front of her and said with a smile, 'How about some good news to cheer you up?'

'Yes, please,' said her wilting patient. 'What is it?'

'I have the results of the tests in front of me that I did when you came the first time, and they are all satisfactory.'

'What were they for?' Simon asked.

'A blood test to check for anaemia or rhesus antibodies was satisfactory, and the blood and urine checks I did for diabetes were also clear. So apart from the morning sickness, you are starting off with a clean slate.'

'Let's hope that it stays that way,' Simon said, taking his wife's hand in his. 'Do you think Emma should give up in the tea rooms altogether until the baby is born?'

'Maybe for these first months while she has the nausea and there is the greater risk of miscarrying it would be a good idea, but once the sickness has abated and the tests are still showing clear, there will be no reason for her to coddle herself. Just don't overdo it, that's all. Now, I'm going to check your blood pressure, Emma.'

When she'd done that Lizzie said, 'At this moment you are fine, so go home and stop worrying. Remember, thanks to Lord Derringham, I'm only a matter of yards away if you have any problems.'

As they got up to go Emma said to Simon, 'Do you have a recipe for home-made ginger biscuits in your big cook book? And what was the other thing, Lizzie, ginger tea?'

He was smiling, relieved that nothing scary had come up during their visit to the clinic, and promised, 'If I haven't, I can soon get them.'

James was back on duty at the surgery, having left Jess in charge of Jolyon and Pollyanna, and life was generally returning to normal, with Laurel and David back from their honeymoon looking bronzed and happy as they took up their respective positions in the surgery once more as nurse and GP.

They called in at the clinic during the lunch-hour to see what the finished article looked like. They'd gone on honeymoon before it had been finished and both were impressed with the facilities it was offering and interested to know that Lady Olivia Derringham was working there on a voluntary basis twice weekly.

When they'd gone James came in and said, 'I've just been back home to check that all is well with Jolly and Polly. I'm going to let Jess take her to school tomorrow. She's happy enough now.'

He was observing her keenly. Lizzie was still staying aloof from him but was pleasant enough, and he thought that the next time he told her how he felt he would make a better job of it, given the chance.

She could feel the intensity of his gaze and asked, 'What?'

'Nothing,' he replied calmly, and went back to his consulting room feeling better for having seen her.

Lizzie kept her promise the following Saturday. The children came for tea and to stay the night. James brought them in the late afternoon and then went home feeling strangely lost.

He wasn't used to having time on his hands like this, he thought. It would have been a good opportunity to have asked Elaine to go over the accounts with him, but he wasn't in the mood for that sort of thing and decided that he would take some exercise, walk up to the moors above the village and back.

The warm colours of autumn were already disappearing he saw as he left the outskirts of the village and the leaves were falling. Soon it would be November 5th and he would do as he'd always done since the children were small, take them to the bonfire on the village green.

It was a special event that everyone who was mobile attended, with the Women's Institute providing hot soup, parkin and treacle toffee in abundance, and this time he was hoping that Lizzie would be with them. The fact that *he* might be the reason if she wasn't was something he wasn't going to contemplate.

He hadn't been sleeping well since she'd slept in his bed and appeared before him in the flimsy nightdress that she'd been in a rush to cover up. His thoughts and desires were making him restless and he had to keep telling himself to get her out of his mind.

She'd made it clear that she wasn't in the market for being a wife of convenience, much as she loved his children, and he had yet to find the right moment to tell her that was far from what he wanted.

He wanted a wife of warm flesh and blood, wanted to give her a child, their child, to make up for the one she'd lost, but he wasn't making much progress towards that end.

It was dark when he got back to Willowmere and as he passed the peace garden and approached the cottage, he smiled at the thought that all those he cherished were sleeping inside.

Lizzie had made them a special fairy tea of tiny sandwiches and cakes with lots of crisps and ice cream, and afterwards the highlight of the occasion had been when Bryan had let them watch the cows being milked in the sheds at the far end of the field at the back of the cottage.

It was lovely having the children, she thought as they

settled down to sleep, one on either side of her, but she'd made James feel he wasn't welcome, which was unforgivable as without him nothing made sense. It would have served her right if he'd refused to let them come, and she wondered what he was doing.

Probably having a well-earned rest, she thought wryly, and no one could blame him for that! James must have little time for himself yet she'd never heard him complain. He'd achieved a degree of contentment that she'd never found, but he had the children to give his life purpose and that must have made all the difference.

The white orchids and roses he'd given her were still fresh and beautiful on her dressing table and she wanted them to last for ever as something to hold on to in the confusion of her feelings for the father of the two innocents beside her.

On Sunday morning Lizzie eased herself carefully out of the bed and went downstairs to make a cup of tea before setting the table for breakfast.

As she sat sipping it in the silence she had a sudden yearning to hear James's voice and picked up the phone, even though it was only half past six.

He answered it immediately and when she spoke he said, 'What's wrong, Lizzie? It's not Jolly, is it?'

'No. Nothing like that,' she told him. 'The children are still asleep and I thought I'd report to base that all is well at camp Carmichael.'

'Right,' he said whimsically, and she could tell he

was smiling. 'You do know that it's only half past six, I take it.'

She was contrite. 'I'm sorry. Were you still asleep?'

'Er...no. I surfaced some time ago.'

He could have told her that he'd been longing to hear her voice after a strange night without Polly and Jolly in the house, and that she was the only person he had ever trusted to have his children overnight. As if she'd read his mind, Lizzie was on the phone, assuring him that all was well.

'They are still asleep,' she assured him once more, 'and as it is Sunday there's no rush, is there? I'll bring them back in the middle of the morning.'

'There is no need for you to do that. I'll come for them, and thanks for having them, Lizzie.'

'It is I who should thank you,' she told him soberly.

'Whatever you say, but don't forget that I'm taking you out for the evening some time soon as a thank-you for being there for both of them when Jolyon had the accident in the playground. In fact, why don't we arrange it now? A weeknight would suit me best as Helen sleeps in during the week and will be there to keep an eye on the children while I'm out.'

'Any evening is all right for me,' she informed him. 'I rarely go out after a day at the clinic, unless it's to walk to the beautiful lake near David and Laurel's house.'

'How about Wednesday then? Not too far off. I'll pick you up about eightish. The children will be fast asleep by then and we'll go for a nice meal somewhere.'

There was silence at the other end of the line and he

sensed her indecision as clearly as if she was standing next to him.

'Yes, all right,' she agreed at last. 'That would be very nice. I hear voices upstairs, do you want a word?'

'If they're awake, yes,' he said evenly, as if he hadn't just had his enthusiasm lessened for them spending some time together in more intimate surroundings than their usual ones.

She could hear small feet on the cottage's narrow staircase and called, 'Your daddy is on the phone, children, and wants to talk to you.' As she went into the kitchen to start preparing their breakfast she could hear them telling James in excited voices how they'd been to see Daisy being milked, and she hoped he was suitably impressed.

Pollyanna and Jolyon had gone. James had picked them up as promised and the empty silence that usually hung over the cottage prevailed once more.

He'd given her a questioning look when he'd arrived and she'd presumed it was because of her lack of eagerness to be alone with him away from their everyday life, but under their present circumstances she could hardly explain that it was uncertainty rather than reluctance that had been the cause of it.

But it wasn't stopping her from deciding that just for once she was going to let him see the Lizzie Carmichael that she used to be in the days when she'd loved and been loved in return.

CHAPTER NINE

THE rest of Sunday passed uneventfully for Lizzie. Weatherwise it was a typical October day with a chill in the air warning that winter was on its way, and with it came Christmas, she thought as she did her usual Sunday chores.

It would be her first one in Willowmere, and it would be lovely to be on the sidelines of the children's excitement. But she didn't visualise much cause for rejoicing on her own account. James's intention to take her out to dine would be out of his usual consideration for anyone that he felt indebted to, and when the festive season arrived he would have the friends who'd always been there for him to share it with.

But she'd had a few quiet Christmas times since she'd lost Richard and another one wouldn't be the end of the world. At least she would be spending it in the beautiful Cheshire countryside.

A few of her patients were expecting their babies during the festive season and that would be something to anticipate with pleasure.

* * *

When James awoke on Monday morning and went to get the children up, he found Pollyanna clomping around in the blue shoes and as he smiled at her he thought that Lizzie had the knack of getting it just right with his children. He wished she would come up with something that was just right for him, such as responding when the chemistry was there between them. Surely she could feel it, too?

There were times when she was near that his need of her was so great he had to exercise self-control or step into the unknown and risk a rebuff. But he had waited a long time to find someone he could love as much as he'd loved Julie, and could wait longer if he had to, if only Lizzie would give him a sign that she cared, but so far it wasn't forthcoming. But there was Wednesday night to look forward to. Would it bring the answer to his dreams, or be just a friendly meeting of acquaintances?

When she answered the doorbell to him on the night in question James's spirits took a downward turn. Lizzie was still in her uniform.

When she saw his expression she said hurriedly, 'I'm sorry. I was called out to a delivery only minutes after I came home.' She stepped back to let him in. 'Is Natalie Morgan one of your patients?'

'Yes. She and her husband have a bed-and-breakfast place halfway up the hill road. So it was Natalie who called you out.'

'Mmm, it was. She'd started labour and was panicking now the time had come, wishing she hadn't arranged to have the baby at home. As it happened, she didn't. I had to get the emergency services out to take her to St Gabriel's. The baby was in distress and I couldn't take any chances. Do you still want to go for the meal? I need to shower and get changed. It will take me at least half an hour.'

'Go ahead. I've booked a table and will ring the restaurant to explain that we'll be delayed.' As she turned towards the stairs, he added, 'That is, if you're not too tired after working all day and then being called out.'

'No, I'm fine,' she said as a lump came up in her throat. She wasn't used to being fussed over, but since coming to Willowmere James had been concerned about her welfare on other occasions too, and it gave her a warm feeling inside. Even though she expected he would be just as caring for anyone he thought was in need of it. But if she'd been dropping in her tracks she wouldn't have wanted to miss the evening that he'd planned so she climbed the narrow staircase and was under the shower within seconds.

There was no need to consider what she was going to wear. She'd laid the clothes out on the bed that morning and when she came downstairs again Lizzie was dressed in semi-eveningwear. A short, low-cut, strappy black dress with a matching jacket draped over her arm to keep at bay the chilly night if needed.

The long golden plait had been untwined and her hair hung down in a shining swathe on her shoulders. As he took in the effect James saw that there was a question in the violet eyes meeting his and wished he knew what it was so that he could give the right answer. That being so, he said what he was thinking, which couldn't possibly be wrong.

'You look wonderful. Heads will turn when we enter the restaurant.'

He saw her colour rise at the compliment but her reply was flippant.

'Why, because I'm showing some cleavage? I can't remember when last I dressed like this.'

'No, not because of that. It will be because you'll be the most attractive woman in the place.'

Lizzie didn't take him up on that. She wanted to calm down now and take the evening in her stride, but the fact that James approved of her appearance was like balm to her soul.

Tonight she wanted to be a woman that he was happy to be with, not someone the children liked, or the midwife who brought babies into the world, but an attractive and interesting companion, and so far she seemed to have got it right.

A little later, as he watched her sparkle like the wine in their glasses James thought he was out of practice at this sort of thing, and so was Lizzie if he wasn't mistaken.

Their social and sex lives had been on hold for a long time because of circumstances they'd had no control over, and the last time he'd taken flowers to Julie's grave in its quiet corner of the churchyard he'd felt as if she was smiling down on him in gentle approval.

But there was nothing to say that Lizzie was feeling the same way. It didn't mean that because he was ready to accept closure she felt the same. Her gaze was on him over the top of her wineglass and the sparkle was dimming into uncertainty.

'Why so serious?' she asked.

She almost dropped the glass when he said gravely, 'Have you ever slept with anyone else since your husband died?'

'No,' she croaked. 'I've never wanted to. Have you?'

'No, for the same reason, I've thought of it once or twice but that was as far as it went.'

'And?' she questioned warily.

He was smiling. 'I've sometimes thought I was crazy, but I don't any more.' The food they'd ordered arrived at that moment, so talking was replaced by eating, and when it could have been resumed during a lull between courses there was silence between them until James asked casually, 'Will you be staying in the village over Christmas?'

'Yes,' she said. 'I have nowhere else that I would wish to be.' *Except near you*, she thought, but said instead, 'I would imagine that Willowmere is quite something then.'

'It is indeed. You will see for yourself when the time comes. We're having a big party at Bracken House in Christmas week so that we can all be together, Helen, Jess, Georgina and Ben, with little Arran this time, and David and Laurel also with us for the first time. I'm still waiting to hear from Anna and Glenn if they're going to be home for Christmas. If they can't be with us, it will not be the same.'

'It sounds lovely,' she said in a tone just as casual as the one he'd used.

'So do you think you might stop by?' he asked. 'The children will want to show you what Santa has brought.'

'Yes, if I'm invited. I wouldn't want to intrude.'

It wouldn't be the first Christmas she'd spent alone. At St Gabriel's she'd always offered to work so that staff with families could be with them.

It went without saying that babies ready to leave the womb were no respecters of holiday times, so someone had to be there to welcome them when they decided to put in an appearance. Even here in Willowmere there might be a birth on Christmas Day or thereabouts.

'Of course you are invited,' he said stiffly, and because she'd been so downbeat about it added perversely, 'The more the merrier. I know two small mortals who will be most disappointed if you're not there.'

'And that's it?'

'No, of course not! I'll be disappointed too, Lizzie.'

'Then I'd better be there, hadn't I?'

'Yes,' he said steadily, 'you had, but Christmas is some weeks off. The next event in the village is the bonfire this coming Saturday. Everyone turns out for that. The Women's Institute excel themselves with the food on that occasion and the Scouts and Guides help out, with their leaders in charge of the fireworks.'

'Sounds good.'

'Yes, it is.' He was beckoning the waiter over to settle the bill and as she waited Lizzie thought what a strange evening it had been. First the disconcerting question about her sex life, or lack of it, then a half-hearted invitation to his Christmas party, and lastly he'd been describing the village bonfire in terms glowing as the fire itself, like a salesman on a front doorstep.

As they got up to go James had a sickening feeling that the evening had not been the success he'd hoped for, and he was to blame. He'd talked about everything except the feelings close to his heart, and Lizzie must think he was deranged.

She had no idea how she'd been arousing his senses in the smart black dress that revealed the smooth skin of her neck and shoulders. He'd seen quite a bit of her on another occasion when she'd been in his bed, cuddling Pollyanna, but at the time he'd been too harassed over Jolyon's accident and Polly's distress to take note. However, it *had* registered in his subconscious.

But tonight it was different. He'd been keen to be alone with her and what had he done? Started off by asking Lizzie about her sex life, like some interfering therapist.

Then just as they had been finishing the meal he'd started to eulogise about the bonfire as if Lizzie would never have seen a pile of wood burning brightly on a November night, when all the time what he should have been doing was telling her how much he wanted her in his life...for always.

There was silence between them again as he drove them back to the village and James thought if she asked him in it would be surprising, yet surprising it was.

'Do you want to come in for a coffee?' she asked, standing in the open door of the cottage.

'No,' he replied abruptly, and she stepped back as if he'd struck her, 'but I'll come in for this.' Stepping over the threshold, he took her in his arms and kissed her brow, her lips and the hollow of her throat until she was clinging to him in total abandonment.

'What was that for?' she gasped when at last he let her go.

He smiled. 'It was to make up for the opportunities I've missed tonight, and now I'm going before I carry you upstairs and we let the chemistry between us really take over. Or are you of the opinion that there isn't any, that I'm mistaken?'

'I don't know what I think,' she said weakly. 'My life has changed so much since I came to Willowmere my mind is in a whirl. The only people who have needed me in the last few years have been my patients, for obvious reasons, but now it is all changing and, James, I think that I need you more than you need me. You are surrounded by people who love and respect you, and you must have been happy enough since you lost your wife or you would have done something about it. Do you really want to change all that?'

'What do you mean?' he said stiffly. 'Do you honestly think it has been easy? My priorities have always been my children and the practice. But as you've just said, one's life can change unexpectedly and then it's decision time, but it sounds to me as if you're trying to talk me out of falling in love with you. That you don't want to break out of the safe cocoon that you've wrapped around you, and so you're reminding me of what a good life I've got.'

He sighed, running his fingers through his dark hair. 'Lizzie. It's us I'm talking about at this moment. Think about what I've said, will you?' With that he opened the door and went out into the night.

As the door swung to behind him she leant against it weakly. Why had she got this mania of wanting to be so sure that James wanted her for herself alone and for no other reason? After the way he'd kissed her she should have no doubts on that score, and yet she'd ended up by trying to dissuade him from changing their relationship from friends into lovers.

Now it was her turn to sigh for the complexities of her thoughts as she went slowly up to bed, knowing there would be little sleep to escape into after what had just happened.

When Olivia Derringham arrived for her Thursday morning voluntary help in the clinic she asked, 'Are you all right, Lizzie? You look pale.'

She managed a smile. Pale was how she felt, pale and pathetic. The man she'd been drawn to since their moment of meeting had offered her a glimpse of heaven on earth the night before, and she'd been dithering like a frightened virgin.

There would be no chance to talk to him alone in the next few days unless she made a big thing of it, but on Saturday after the bonfire she was going to tell him how much she cared, hoping that he hadn't taken her humming and hawing too much to heart. In the meantime there were babies to weigh and mothers to advise on feeding and teething, and for those who were waiting to be blessed with a newborn the meticulous checks for such things as rising blood pressure, diabetes and other complications of pregnancy.

Thankfully, and it wasn't always the case, it was a smooth run and, when lunchtime came she went across to the surgery kitchen to make a mug of tea to drink with the sandwich she'd brought. Hoping at the same time that she might see James.

But as if she'd read her mind, as she was passing the nurses' room Laurel said that he'd gone on an urgent visit to someone staying at The Pheasant who'd developed severe chest pains and couldn't get his breath.

'Yes,' David chipped in from behind her. 'A couple of elderly walking fanatics are booked in there for a few days and it sounds as if the old guy has been overdoing it.' Then he said the same thing that Helen had said. 'You look pale, Lizzie. Are you all right?'

'I'm fine in body,' she told him, 'but the mind is a bit cluttered at the moment.'

'Anything I can help with?' he asked.

She shook her head. 'No, thanks just the same, David. It is something I have to sort out myself.'

The man that James had been called out to needed an ambulance with all speed, he decided when he entered a chintzy bedroom beneath the eaves of The Pheasant. He was gasping for breath, perspiring heavily, and there was froth on his blue lips.

When James sounded his heart it was beating fast and

irregularly and he reached for his mobile and made the call to the emergency services, thinking as he did so that it had all the signs of a heart attack except for the frothiness of his lips, which could indicate some kind of poisoning.

The sick man's wife was waiting anxiously beside the bed and when he'd finished phoning she said, 'Is it his heart, Doctor?'

'It could be,' he said gravely. 'All the symptoms are there, including the blueness around the mouth, but I'm not sure about the frothiness. Has your husband eaten anything that could have poisoned his system this morning?'

There was horror in her expression as she listened to what he was saying and she gasped, 'We were up on the tops first thing among the gorse and heather and we saw what looked as if there were some wildberries still around, and as I've often made a fruit tart with them he gathered some and ate them, even though I warned him that they weren't growing as close to the ground as they usually do. So maybe he was mistaken, is that what you're saying?'

'It's possible,' he said with continuing gravity, 'and whatever they were may have poisoned him.'

The screeching of a siren announced that the ambulance had arrived, and as he heard them come in down below he went to the top of the stairs and called, 'Up here, quickly!'

When they appeared he explained briefly the possibility of poisoning from unidentified wildberries, and after giving him oxygen to help his breathing and checking his blood pressure, as James had already done, they carried him quickly to the ambulance and set off in the quiet morning, with his wife ashen-faced beside him and sirens blaring once more.

James headed back to the surgery, glancing towards Lizzie's domain as he went to his room, but he didn't knock on her door, much as he would have liked to. Every one of the events of the night before were crystal clear and every time he thought about her, passionate and un-resisting in his arms, he longed to hold her close again, but there was the aftermath of that passion to consider and he didn't know how he would cope if he couldn't have her. She had brightened his life and loved his children almost as much as he did. Until last night he'd seen the way ahead clearly, but Lizzie's hesitancy had shattered the dream and he was going to stay away from her until she was ready to tell him truthfully what was in her mind.

As she got ready to go to the bonfire on Saturday night Lizzie was wondering if James would be expecting her to be there after Wednesday night. She'd spent the afternoon in the nearest town, doing some clothes shopping to take her mind off what she was going to say when she saw him, and the thought kept recurring that it wasn't going to be the most romantic setting in which to tell him that she loved him, with fireworks screeching above, the fire cracking noisily beside them and the children close by, but for some perverse reason she didn't care. It would be easier in a public place, and she wasn't exactly going to be making the announcement over the loudspeaker system.

Dressing in a warm sweater with a thick jacket over it, and jeans, boots and a woolly hat on her head, she thought that her attire was very different from Wednesday night's. She doubted it would have the same effect on James as that had.

When she stepped out of the cottage into the cold night air there were lots of people about, all moving in the direction of the playing field in the park that ran alongside the river bank, and she thought that this was what living in the countryside was all about—a feeling of community, a common interest.

She loved this place, but she loved the man who had held her in his arms on Wednesday night more. She loved his children too, and would count it a rich blessing to be part of their lives. But first she had to find out if James had really meant the things he'd said the last time they were together.

When she arrived at the bonfire there were so many people there that she had difficulty finding him and the children. Sarah was there with her fiancé, happily looking forward to the wedding that had been put forward to next Saturday, and she saw Jess in the crowd with her sturdy farmer's son and wondered if he would persuade her to emigrate like he wanted to.

A voice behind her in the crowd asked, 'Are you looking for James?' When she turned Helen was there, holding a tray of parkin and smiling her welcome for the woman who she hoped was going to be the new mistress of Bracken House.

Unaware of the direction of the housekeeper's

thoughts, Lizzie nodded, knowing she wouldn't be heard above the noise, and the other woman pointed to the far end of the field and she saw that James was there with the children on either side of him.

When she was just a few feet away Jolyon saw her and cried, 'There's Lizzie.' And when Polly heard him she let go of James's hand and came running towards her, with Jolyon following at a slower pace. As Lizzie took their hands in turn and began to walk towards him, James watched her gravely.

'Hello, there,' he said in the kind of tone he'd used when they'd first met, and her spirits sank as she thought, *Is this how it is going to be, back to square one?*

But there was no sign of her inner doubts as she called a casual 'Hello' across the intervening space.

'How long have you been here?' he asked.

'Only a matter of minutes,' she replied as the three of them joined him a safe distance away from the fire. 'What a crowd!'

'There always is,' he told her. A firework exploded into bright stars high above them. 'A lot of work goes into it by the Willowmere Events Committee, and it's the same at Christmas.'

She didn't want to be involved in all this small talk, Lizzie was thinking. She wanted to talk about them, and as the numbers increased of those around the fire she was deciding that it hadn't been a good idea to contemplate telling James that she loved him on an occasion such as this.

They could have talked at Bracken House or the

cottage, but she'd wanted it to be on neutral ground, and as she looked around her she thought it couldn't be more neutral than this.

As the children watched the spectacle goggle-eyed, James said in a low voice, 'So why are you here, Lizzie? Is it to finish your downbeat comments of the other night?'

'No,' she told him quietly. 'As far as I'm concerned, what I have to say is as upbeat as it can get.' Her gaze locked with his, and she said, with eyes melting with love for him, 'I've come to tell you...'

Her voice trailed away as above the noise of the bonfire a voice cried, 'James! Surprise! Surprise! We're back!' A woman who'd been pushing her way through the crowd, with a man who was deeply tanned by her side, flung herself into James's arms, while Polly and Jolly clung to her skirts, crying excitedly, 'Anna!'

Aware of how much joy the moment was bringing, and that James had forgotten she was there in that moment of reunion, Lizzie stepped back into the shadow of the bushes, and as the cries of delight continued to ring out she slipped away, deciding that such moments were to be treasured by the family concerned without strangers hanging around.

She saw Helen again as she was leaving, talking to Jess and her boyfriend, and stopped to inform them that Anna was home from Africa, then went on her way with their delighted cries ringing in her ears too. She felt more alone than she'd ever been in her life before.

It had been a repetition of that time in the hospital when she'd been feeling secure in James's need of her and Helen and Jess had arrived and unwittingly brought her back down to earth.

How could she have ever imagined herself as part of that secure, loving family circle that she'd just witnessed? she thought as she sat in her sitting room, staring into space, with the noise of the fireworks in the distance. She hadn't been wrong when she'd told James that *he* didn't need *her* as much as *she* needed *him*.

Lizzie didn't see anything of James and the children over the rest of the weekend, but didn't expect to. They would all have lots to talk about and Anna and Glenn would have to settle in again after their absence from the place where she and James had been brought up.

The children would be so happy and excited to have their aunt back, she thought, which was only right as Anna had put her own life on hold to fill the gap that the death of their mother had left in theirs when they had been only a few weeks old.

From the way she'd greeted them it seemed reasonable to expect that she would want to take up where she'd left off, the only difference being that her sacrifices hadn't been in vain. Anna had at last been reunited with and married the only man she'd ever loved, and it made Lizzie think that James had only ever loved one person too and probably still did, which made how he'd kissed her, and what he'd said to her, seem even more like just a moment of madness.

* * *

She was wrong in thinking that James wouldn't notice her absence. As Anna had released him from her embrace to hold the children close in those moments of homecoming, he'd turned to introduce Lizzie to the unexpected arrivals and saw that she'd gone.

He'd groaned silently, saying nothing that would take away the joy of their homecoming for his sister and her husband, but there was the knowledge that Lizzie had been prevented from finishing what she had to say to him, and that was the last thing he would have wanted to happen as it could have been the words he'd been longing to hear.

But instead she'd left the scene as if she'd felt like an intruder, and she would never be that. At the first opportunity he was going to tell her so in no uncertain terms.

He'd waited so long for someone like her to come into his life that he could not afford to lose her, but for the present there was Anna bubbling over with happiness to be back, with Glenn watching over her adoringly, and for a little while he was going to put his own affairs on the back burner until the right moment occurred. He was determined to make sure it wasn't long in coming.

CHAPTER TEN

DAVID TRELAWNEY'S new wife, Laurel, had come into the practice as a temporary nurse on the arrangement that it might be just until Anna came back. Before she'd married Glenn Hamilton there had been two nurses at the practice—Beth Jackson, who had been full time, and Anna on part-time hours because of her involvement with the children.

When she'd gone to work in Africa with Glenn, Gillian had taken her place on a full-time basis, and shortly afterwards another vacancy had occurred when Beth had left to open a delicatessen in the village with her husband, and a very successful venture it was turning out to be.

It was then that Laurel, who had previously been a nurse in a big London hospital, had joined the practice and in the days that followed Anna's return she was anxious to find out what was going to happen.

If Anna wanted her job back on a full-time arrangement, which she might, then she, Laurel, would not be required. Witnessing the other woman's pleasure in returning to the place where she'd put down her roots seemed to indicate that job hunting might soon be on the cards for herself, and she didn't want that.

She loved the idea of David and herself working in the same place in health care and didn't want to have to leave, but told herself she'd known the score when she'd taken the job and would have to abide by it.

They'd had David's friend Lizzie Carmichael round one night for supper and had asked her what she thought was going to happen now that Anna was back, but she'd known no more than they did about what was going on at Bracken House since Anna's return. All she could say was that on the few occasions she'd seen James since his sister's return, he'd been pleasant enough, but had made no attempts to speak to her privately.

David was just as anxious as Laurel about her position at the practice after a week of uncertainty while Anna and Glenn wallowed in the peace of Willowmere after the frenetic pace of their life in Africa, and when he asked James if he knew what Anna's plans were, he shook his head.

'I've been giving them time to settle back into our way of life,' he told him, 'but over the weekend am going to have a sorting out. I'm going to offer Glenn a partnership in the practice, and you too, if you would be interested, David. If Glenn accepts, it will leave Ben Allardyce free to go back to the paediatric surgery he's been missing out on while he's been helping to cover Georgina's maternity leave. If Georgina decides to come back to us when her leave is up, I intend to offer her a partnership too, which should leave the surgery well blessed with doctors.'

'I'd be delighted to accept your offer,' David said immediately.

'Good. But it doesn't answer your question about what Anna plans to do, does it? As I've said, I'm going to discuss it with her over the weekend and should know where Laurel stands in the scheme of things by Monday morning, if that is all right with you.'

When David had gone, James thought there was no one more anxious to sort some things out than he was, but it wasn't all with regard to the practice.

Since the night of the bonfire he'd seen Lizzie going in and out of the clinic a few times and had had to restrain himself from stopping her and sorting their lives out on the spot, but he was forcing himself to wait until the weekend after he'd spoken to Anna and Glenn, and it was not easy.

For one thing, in spite of the excitement of their aunt's return the children kept asking for Lizzie. 'Why doesn't she come to see us any more?' Jolyon had asked one night when the bedtime story had been read.

Pollyanna had put in her plea by saying, 'I love Lizzie.'

Don't we all? he'd thought achingly every time he imagined how she must have felt when she'd disappeared from the bonfire. Come another Saturday he was going to find out once and for all if they had a future together.

It was great to have Glenn and Anna back in Willowmere, but if there was any justice in the world his future and that of Pollyanna and Jolyon was with

Lizzie. He just hoped that when it came to question time she would have the answer he was praying for.

After breakfast on Saturday the children went upstairs to play and as Anna and Glenn got up from the table he said, 'Could I have a word with you folks?'

'Sure,' Glenn said, and Anna nodded her agreement.

'I've got a couple of things I want to ask you both,' he said with a gravity that had them both sitting down again.

'First of all, would you be interested in a partnership in the practice, Glenn? You weren't with us long before you married Anna and went away, but it was long enough to know that you are an exceptionally good doctor, as is David Trelawney, the other GP in the practice. I've offered him a partnership too if he wants it and he is keen to accept. So how would *you* feel about joining us on a permanent basis as well?'

There was silence for a moment and then Glenn said, 'I am most interested in your offer, James.' He glanced at his wife. 'And I know that Anna won't object. She tells me frequently that there is nowhere else she wants to live except here in Willowmere. So, yes, definitely, I accept your offer.'

'That's fantastic!' James exclaimed. 'And now it's your turn, Anna. Do you want your old job back?'

'No,' she said. 'As you know, James, I can't have children because of the injuries I received when Julie and I were in that dreadful accident. So we're going to adopt a child, or two if they'll let us, and I'll want to be there for them all the time as they get used to new parents and surroundings. I hope you don't mind.'

'Of course I don't mind!' he exclaimed. 'That's wonderful news.'

'I know that adoption can be a lengthy procedure but while we're waiting I will enjoy having some time to myself, which could mean that I won't be there for Pollyanna and Jolyon as much as I used to be, I'm afraid,' she said apologetically.

'You don't need to worry about that at all, and especially if a certain community midwife agrees to marry me,' he told her. 'I'm in love with her, the children love her too, and she loves them. Her name is Lizzie, short for Elizabeth, Carmichael. She lost her husband three years ago in similar circumstances to how I lost Julie and thinks that I don't really need her because I'm so well blessed with family and friends. So I've got to convince her that her place is here at Bracken House with me as my wife. Wish me luck, will you?'

Anna stared at him in delighted astonishment. 'That's the best news I've heard in years. How can I meet this amazing woman who has broken through the James Bartlett barrier? We're not talking about the blonde midwife who's based next door, are we? I haven't met her yet, but I've seen her coming and going.'

'Yes, we are,' he told her, adding with a smile, 'How many community midwives do you think we have in Willowmere? Lizzie is the one and only at the moment.'

'So when are you going to pop the question?' Anna wanted to know.

'Soon, very soon—today, I hope. She is the only woman I've looked at twice since I lost Julie and I'm in love with her, but first I've got to convince her how much I need her. Lizzie thinks that because I'm surrounded by loving family and friends she'll be on the fringe of things if she marries me. She was beside me at the bonfire when you surprised me, and when I turned round to introduce her to you, she'd gone.

'She's had a grim time in her private life over recent years and is wary of relationships for the wrong reasons, but the first chance I get I'm going round to her cottage to ask her to marry me. So would you mind keeping an eye on the children for me while I'm there?'

'Of course we will,' they chorused, and Glenn said, 'We've got some news for *you*. We've put a deposit on a house in the village.'

'Great!' he cried. 'Which one?'

'Mistletoe Cottage, next to the water-mill.'

'This is going to be a day to remember,' James said. 'I've got myself two new partners, which means I can sit back sometimes and spend time with Lizzie if she'll have me, and you folks are putting down some fresh roots in Willowmere in that delightful cottage. This is simply wonderful.'

By the late afternoon James was beginning to feel that things weren't quite so wonderful. Every time he'd been round to Lizzie's she hadn't been there, and he kept telling himself that if he'd had any sense he should have let her know he was coming. It was a form of arrogance to expect her to be there just because he'd decided to honour her with his presence.

He was turning away on his last abortive visit when he heard a faint cry and stopped in his tracks. It came again and his blood ran cold. The door was locked. He'd tried it a few times and was going to look a fool if he broke it down and then found that the calls for help were coming from somewhere else.

But he wasn't taking any chances, he decided. He'd lost one woman he adored and now the kind fates had brought Lizzie into his life. He wasn't going to lose her too if he could help it, and as the cry for help came again he put his shoulder to the door.

Lizzie was lying in a crumpled heap at the bottom of the narrow staircase and the scene in front of him told its own story. She'd fallen down it.

Her face was twisted with pain and streaked with tears as she cried his name in blessed relief. 'How long have you been here?' he asked gently as he knelt beside her in the confined space.

'For hours,' she sobbed. 'I tripped over the hem of my robe as I was coming downstairs what seems like a lifetime ago, and I can't get up, James.

'I knocked myself out and when I came to couldn't move because I think I've fractured my hip. I've kept drifting off with the pain and then coming back to reality again, and it happened that this time I heard you knocking and ringing the bell. Have you been before?'

'Have I been before?' he repeated gently. 'Yes, I have, my darling. I've been going crazy, desperate to talk to you but without success, and all the time you were lying here.'

Even as he was speaking he was ringing the emergency services and while he asked for an ambulance Lizzie lay white-faced and tear-stained beside him.

His was the name she'd called every time she'd come to. He was the only one she would ever want during good times or bad, and she said weakly, 'I knew you would come.'

He groaned. 'It took me long enough, didn't it?'

'You must have come before when I was out of it.'

'Possibly, but thank God I've found you.'

He'd placed his jacket over her when he'd found her but even so she was shivering from shock and he said quickly, 'Is there a hot-water bottle anywhere in this place?'

'Yes, in the bathroom.'

He looked down at her with all the love in the world in his eyes and said, 'Don't move an inch while I'm getting it.'

'I won't. I can't,' she told him, and he went up the offending stairs like a bullet out of a gun.

When he placed it in her arms she managed a pale smile and said, 'You are so good at taking care of me.'

'I want to do it permanently. That is what I've kept coming round to tell you. Will you let me?'

'Even if I end up walking with a stick?'

'Even if you end up walking with two sticks. Will you marry me, Elizabeth Carmichael? My children and I love you so much. Polly and Jolly keep asking for you. We want you in our lives for always.'

'Do you really?' she said on a sob. 'Then I'd better say yes, hadn't I?'

He could hear the ambulance coming up the road and he kissed her tear-stained cheek. 'Yes, you *had* better say yes, and it will be the sweetest sound I ever heard.'

He phoned Bracken House while the ambulance was on its way to St Gabriel's to let Anna and Glenn know what was happening and warned them that it could be some time before he came back. They were horrified to hear what had happened and Anna said, 'Just do what you have to do, look after Lizzie.'

'I will,' he promised grimly as he held her hand in the ambulance.

It had been nerve-racking, trying to move her out of the small space at the bottom of the stairs without causing further damage to her hip, but the paramedics were skilled in such situations and now she was lying on her good side in the ambulance, with him watching over her like a guardian angel.

An X-ray showed a fracture of the neck of the femur and that luckily the bone ends hadn't become impacted in the fall. An operation would be necessary to realign them and until it was performed the pain would persist and she wouldn't be able to walk. But once it had been satisfactorily accomplished she should soon become mobile again.

The deep cut on her head from when she'd hit the floor in the hall had been stitched, and no bleeding inside the skull had shown up, as it had with Jolyon, so the damage to her femur was the main problem.

As they were taking her to Theatre she said drowsily, 'Go home to the children, James. I'll ask them to let you know when it's over and I'm in the high dependency ward, or wherever else they decide to put me.'

He shook his head. 'Polly and Jolly will be fine. They're with Anna and Glenn, who are most sorry to hear what has happened. I'm not budging, Lizzie.' And with his voice deepening, he went on, 'Never in my wildest dreams did I think I would be proposing to you while you were in a heap at the bottom of those stupid stairs, but I got the answer I was longing for. So I want to ask you now, my darling, how would you like a Christmas wedding?'

'Mmm,' she murmured as they wheeled her into Theatre, and as the doors closed behind her James thought wretchedly that this was a repeat of the awful moment when Jolly had been hurt. He couldn't wait for the four of them to be together in more tranquil times.

Surgery on Lizzie's broken hip had gone smoothly, the orthopaedic surgeon who had operated told James when he came to see him afterwards. He confirmed that the bone ends at the neck of the femur had been realigned and metal screws inserted to keep them in position. In a few days' time she would be able to walk without pain and return to normal living.

'I was surprised to see Lizzie Carmichael on the table,' he said. 'I knew her when she worked here. What connection does she have with you?'

'We're going to be married,' James told him.

'Really! You must have something special to have captured Lizzie. There were a few guys here who tried to get to know her but she was never interested.'

'I consider myself very fortunate.'

'Yes, I'm sure you do, but we're not going to let you have her back too soon. She was lying injured for a long time and we'll be watching for the effects of shock for a couple of days, as well as making sure she's mobile before we discharge her. If you want to be there for her when she comes round, they've taken her to the recovery unit.'

If he wanted to be there for her! James thought as he strode off in that direction. *That was all he was ever going to want, to be there for Lizzie...and his children.*

When she came round from the anaesthetic and saw him sitting beside the bed, holding her hand, she said weakly, 'Break it to me gently. What is it to be, James? One stick or two?'

'Neither, from what I can gather,' he told her gently. 'You might need some support for a little while but nothing permanent, and when they discharge you, you're coming to Bracken House where you can be looked after properly.'

'I thought we weren't supposed to see each other before the wedding, that it's bad luck?'

He was smiling down at her. 'All our bad luck is going to be a thing of the past from now on, you'll see.'

She managed a smile of her own and as a nurse appeared at the bedside, about to suggest that he let the patient get some rest, she said, 'I think you might just be right about that.'

By the time he'd got to the door she'd drifted off again and as he drove back to Willowmere through the dark November night the thought of the joy that this particular Christmas was going to bring took away some of the nightmare that the day had brought.

Lizzie was discharged three days later and as she walked slowly up the drive of Bracken House, holding on to James, she could scarcely believe that this gracious dwelling was going to be her home from now on.

During the past three years there'd been the soulless apartment across the way from St Gabriel's, and here in Willowmere the small cottage with the narrow staircase that had been her undoing. Neither of them could compare even remotely with Bracken House, and to live there with James and the children would be bliss.

But first Pollyanna and Jolyon had to be told what the new arrangement was going to be, and the last thing she wanted was for them to be made to feel insecure because of it.

They knew she loved them and they loved her in return, but not yet as someone who would very soon be sleeping in the same bed as their father. Until they were married she was going to occupy the bed in the spare room next to theirs, and she and James had decided that when the twins came home from school they would tell them about her coming to live with them and the changes that would be taking place at Christmas time.

Helen had made lunch for the two of them and was beaming at them as she observed how James was looking at Lizzie. She would have a perm for the wedding, she decided happily…and a new hat…

Anna and Glenn were nowhere to be seen. They'd moved into rented property at the other end of the village until the purchase of Mistletoe Cottage was completed, so as to give Lizzie space during her first weeks at Bracken House, but it wasn't stopping Anna from being eager to make friends with the woman who had brought her brother out from behind the defences he'd erected since losing Julie.

Jess tactfully disappeared when she'd brought the children home from school, and when they came in and saw Lizzie they smiled but didn't come rushing up to her as they usually did, and she found herself tensing. Had she been taking too much for granted? she thought.

Jolyon spoke the first. 'Which is your poorly leg?' he asked with his usual attention to detail.

'This one,' she said softly, pointing to the leg in question.

'Won't you be able to play with us any more?' was Pollyanna's contribution to the conversation.

'Of course I will,' she told them. 'We'll have lots of fun.'

'Lizzie is coming to live with us. What do you think about that?' James said.

'Is it because we haven't got a mummy?' asked the deeper thinker of the two.

'No,' Lizzie said before James could answer him. 'It's because I love you all and you all love me, but I'll be able to do all the things for you that a mummy would do, and you would like that, wouldn't you? So am I going to get a kiss?'

'Yes!' they cried together, and as they ran towards her James met Lizzie's gaze above their small fair heads and the message was there for all time in the eyes looking into his.

I love you all, it said.

Lizzie had been absent from the clinic for a week and during that time one of the practice nurses who'd been involved with antenatal matters at the surgery before the new clinic had opened had dealt with patients' health checks and problems, but there was relief all round when she appeared once more in her neat blue uniform and with a solitaire diamond ring on her engagement finger.

When she told them the news, there were excited congratulations from all sides and Helen said, 'I've thought all along that you and James were made for each other, but do I take it that you needed convincing?'

'Something like that,' Lizzie told her blithely, with the memory new and precious of how they'd gone to a jeweller's in the town and together had chosen the beautiful ring. Every time she looked down at it on her finger, the wedding they were planning for Christmas Eve couldn't come quickly enough.

While she'd waited for James to come for her on that special day there had been a poignant moment in the midst of her happiness when she'd taken off the wedding ring that Richard had placed on her finger all that time ago. She would never forget him, just as James would never forget Julie, but they were both being given a second chance of happiness and Richard would never want to deny her that.

The news that James Bartlett had succumbed at last, and to the new community midwife of all people, had gone out on the bush telegraph with all speed after one of the expectant mothers visiting the clinic had heard the conversation. When they'd heard the news, all the hopefuls had sighed and wondered what she'd got that they hadn't!

Anna was to be matron of honour at the wedding, Pollyanna bridesmaid, and Jolyon had dubiously agreed to be a page boy. Glenn was James's choice for best man, and the only vacancy amongst those taking part was someone to give Lizzie away.

When the question arose she told James serenely, *'I'm the one who's giving myself to you, no one else, and shall walk down the aisle to stand beside you at the altar on my own as I've been for so long, and after that I will never be alone again, will I, James?'*

'You can count on that,' he told her tenderly, and that was how it was going to be.

The day they had both been waiting for had dawned, and when the curtains had been drawn back at Bracken House there had been cries of delight from everyone. Snow had fallen during the night and the village lay beneath a smooth white blanket.

When noon came Edwina Crabtree and her friends

would send the bells pealing out joyfully over the village to salute the doctors they all knew as friends. After the wedding, the party at Bracken House that was usually held earlier in Christmas week was going to take place, and this time it would be hosted by James and his new wife.

It was all going as planned, and as villagers and guests in the crowded church waited for the bride to appear, Helen, in one of the front pews, nodded her newly permed locks in satisfaction, and Jess, in love herself, prayed that one day she might be as happy as the little family that she had been delighted to serve...

When Lizzie walked down the aisle to the man she loved, beautiful in a flatteringly simple dress of cream brocade, with a pale fur wrap around her shoulders, she was minus a veil, but in her hair she wore white orchids and pink roses, and was carrying a bouquet of the same flowers as a reminder of the day when James had given her the same kind of delicate blooms.

For the groom and his bride it was as if their worlds had righted themselves, and with the small bridesmaid and page boy happily watching they made their vows with the church bells pealing out joyously over the village.

It was evening and the guests were arriving for the party. Caterers had been hired to prepare a buffet. A giant spruce with bright baubles and coloured lights dominated one corner of the sitting room, and beside it Lizzie and James held hands with the children on either side of them.

He bent and whispered in her ear, 'I love you.'

She gazed up at him with happy tears sparkling on her

lashes and told him, 'I love you too, James, so very much.'

Everyone came to wish the newlyweds well. Anna and Glenn were there, happy to be home and delighted that James had found someone to love as much as he'd loved Julie. Helen and Jess were also beaming their approval, and Georgina and Ben had just arrived with baby Arran in his father's arms. David and Laurel had come with Elaine her aunt, who was practice manager, and next to them were Beth and her husband, away from the deli for a few hours. Gillian the practice nurse had brought her husband, Lord Derringham's estate manager, and last but not least by any means came the Derringhams themselves. It was as if the whole of Willowmere was there to share in the happiness of the Bartlett family.

Later, much later, when the children were fast sleep and the guests had gone, Lizzie lay in her new husband's arms in the bed that she'd once shared with Pollyanna and said dreamily, 'Do you think we might have a baby of our own one day, James?'

'I think that could be arranged,' he said softly. 'A baby for the midwife who has brought so many into the world, and the doctor who would love to see her holding a child of her own in her arms.'

'And a brother or sister for the two adorable children that they love so much already,' she reminded him.

'But of course,' he said. 'That goes without saying.'

MILLS & BOON

SEPTEMBER 2009 HARDBACK TITLES

ROMANCE

A Bride for His Majesty's Pleasure	Penny Jordan
The Master Player	Emma Darcy
The Infamous Italian's Secret Baby	Carole Mortimer
The Millionaire's Christmas Wife	Helen Brooks
Duty, Desire and the Desert King	Jane Porter
Royal Love-Child, Forbidden Marriage	Kate Hewitt
One-Night Mistress...Convenient Wife	Anne McAllister
Prince of Montéz, Pregnant Mistress	Sabrina Philips
The Count of Castelfino	Christina Hollis
Beauty and the Billionaire	Barbara Dunlop
Crowned: The Palace Nanny	Marion Lennox
Christmas Angel for the Billionaire	Liz Fielding
Under the Boss's Mistletoe	Jessica Hart
Jingle-Bell Baby	Linda Goodnight
The Magic of a Family Christmas	Susan Meier
Mistletoe & Marriage	Patricia Thayer & Donna Alward
Her Baby Out of the Blue	Alison Roberts
A Doctor, A Nurse: A Christmas Baby	Amy Andrews

HISTORICAL

Devilish Lord, Mysterious Miss	Annie Burrows
To Kiss a Count	Amanda McCabe
The Earl and the Governess	Sarah Elliott

MEDICAL™

Country Midwife, Christmas Bride	Abigail Gordon
Greek Doctor: One Magical Christmas	Meredith Webber
Spanish Doctor, Pregnant Midwife	Anne Fraser
Expecting a Christmas Miracle	Laura Iding

0809 Gen Std LP

™MILLS & BOON®

SEPTEMBER 2009 LARGE PRINT TITLES

ROMANCE

The Sicilian Boss's Mistress	Penny Jordan
Pregnant with the Billionaire's Baby	Carole Mortimer
The Venadicci Marriage Vengeance	Melanie Milburne
The Ruthless Billionaire's Virgin	Susan Stephens
Italian Tycoon, Secret Son	Lucy Gordon
Adopted: Family in a Million	Barbara McMahon
The Billionaire's Baby	Nicola Marsh
Blind-Date Baby	Fiona Harper

HISTORICAL

Lord Braybrook's Penniless Bride	Elizabeth Rolls
A Country Miss in Hanover Square	Anne Herries
Chosen for the Marriage Bed	Anne O'Brien

MEDICAL™

The Children's Doctor's Special Proposal	Kate Hardy
English Doctor, Italian Bride	Carol Marinelli
The Doctor's Baby Bombshell	Jennifer Taylor
Emergency: Single Dad, Mother Needed	Laura Iding
The Doctor Claims His Bride	Fiona Lowe
Assignment: Baby	Lynne Marshall

MILLS & BOON®

OCTOBER 2009 HARDBACK TITLES

ROMANCE

The Billionaire's Bride of Innocence	Miranda Lee
Dante: Claiming His Secret Love-Child	Sandra Marton
The Sheikh's Impatient Virgin	Kim Lawrence
His Forbidden Passion	Anne Mather
The Mistress of His Manor	Catherine George
Ruthless Greek Boss, Secretary Mistress	Abby Green
Cavelli's Lost Heir	Lynn Raye Harris
The Blackmail Baby	Natalie Rivers
Da Silva's Mistress	Tina Duncan
The Twelve-Month Marriage Deal	Margaret Mayo
And the Bride Wore Red	Lucy Gordon
Her Desert Dream	Liz Fielding
Their Christmas Family Miracle	Caroline Anderson
Snowbound Bride-to-Be	Cara Colter
Her Mediterranean Makeover	Claire Baxter
Confidential: Expecting!	Jackie Braun
Snowbound: Miracle Marriage	Sarah Morgan
Christmas Eve: Doorstep Delivery	Sarah Morgan

HISTORICAL

Compromised Miss	Anne O'Brien
The Wayward Governess	Joanna Fulford
Runaway Lady, Conquering Lord	Carol Townend

MEDICAL™

Hot-Shot Doc, Christmas Bride	Joanna Neil
Christmas at Rivercut Manor	Gill Sanderson
Falling for the Playboy Millionaire	Kate Hardy
The Surgeon's New-Year Wedding Wish	Laura Iding

0909 Gen Std LP

OCTOBER 2009 LARGE PRINT TITLES

ROMANCE

The Billionaire's Bride of Convenience	Miranda Lee
Valentino's Love-Child	Lucy Monroe
Ruthless Awakening	Sara Craven
The Italian Count's Defiant Bride	Catherine George
Outback Heiress, Surprise Proposal	Margaret Way
Honeymoon with the Boss	Jessica Hart
His Princess in the Making	Melissa James
Dream Date with the Millionaire	Melissa McClone

HISTORICAL

His Reluctant Mistress	Joanna Maitland
The Earl's Forbidden Ward	Bronwyn Scott
The Rake's Inherited Courtesan	Ann Lethbridge

MEDICAL™

A Family For His Tiny Twins	Josie Metcalfe
One Night With Her Boss	Alison Roberts
Top-Notch Doc, Outback Bride	Melanie Milburne
A Baby for the Village Doctor	Abigail Gordon
The Midwife and the Single Dad	Gill Sanderson
The Playboy Firefighter's Proposal	Emily Forbes

millsandboon.co.uk Community

Join Us!

The Community is the perfect place to meet and chat to kindred spirits who love books and reading as much as you do, but it's also the place to:

- Get the inside scoop from authors about their latest books
- Learn how to write a romance book with advice from our editors
- Help us to continue publishing the best in women's fiction
- Share your thoughts on the books we publish
- Befriend other users

Forums: Interact with each other as well as authors, editors and a whole host of other users worldwide.

Blogs: Every registered community member has their own blog to tell the world what they're up to and what's on their mind.

Book Challenge: We're aiming to read 5,000 books and have joined forces with The Reading Agency in our inaugural Book Challenge.

Profile Page: Showcase yourself and keep a record of your recent community activity.

Social Networking: We've added buttons at the end of every post to share via digg, Facebook, Google, Yahoo, technorati and de.licio.us.

www.millsandboon.co.uk